InSight of the SEER

Linda Andersson
Sara Marx

Bella
BOOKS
2011

Bella Books, Inc.
P.O. Box 10543
Tallahassee, FL 32302

Printed in the United States of America on acid-free paper
First published 2011

Editor: Katherine V. Forrest
Cover Designer: Linda Callaghan

ISBN 13:978-1-59493-227-4

Photo Credits:
Front cover overlay shows Deborah Stewart from "The Seer."
Photo credit: Jeff Bollman.
Back cover photo of Deborah Stewart and Amanda Majkrzak from "InSight." Photo Credit: Linda Andersson

Linda's Dedications:

To Teri... of course.

To Mom, you thought it would be easy having only one child.

Deborah Stewart, my creative muse and friend. Guin would not be the same without you.

Sara, for taking on this project with me and being so creative and prolific. You are truly talented.

All of the cast and crew from "The Seer" and "InSight." and my friends for their years of support.

Sara's Dedications:

To Linda. Thanks for making me write this.

To my family, especially Macy and Christian. Whatta ball club.

To Roxy. (I'm sure this will be in the report.)

To Mary. So many things to say. Don't worry, I'll say them all...

From Linda and Sara:

Thank you Karin Kallmaker and Linda Hill for being so quickly receptive to our project. Your enthusiasm for fun, sexy literature is inspiring.

Thank you Katherine V. Forrest for being an amazing sounding board and editor. We were your fans long before you became our editor. We won't lie—we freaked out when we got you.

And of course, thank you Teri Maher for being our first set of eyes. You have such a good soul.

About The Authors

Linda Andersson is a writer and filmmaker in Hollywood, CA. Her writer/director credits include, "The Seer," "InSight." and "The 6 Month Rule" among others. Besides writing, she enjoys cooking and the outdoors.

Sara, her partner, a handful of kids and nutty animals live in a tiny beachside town in Southwest Florida where she loves to cook, kayak, spend time at the beach and write, write, write...

Linda and Sara became writing partners after being friends for several years. They originally met when Linda cast Sara in her short film "Misconception" and later "Mood Swing." Both films traveled the LGBT film festival circuit. To keep up with Linda and Sara, please visit: www.watchtheseer.com.

CHAPTER ONE

The last wave of sweltering temperatures had swept through the San Fernando Valley and left residents exhausted in its balmy wake. In a tiny rented pool house behind a trumped-up modern villa, Officer Guin Marcus rifled through her closet on a quest for a uniform with long sleeves. It was day one of her return to work after a dreary month-long mandatory vacation. She grabbed her wrinkled blues, located an ancient clothes iron and headed for the kitchen.

She flipped back the top of the coffeemaker. A long-expired filter brimming with moldy grounds stared back at her. She grimaced, dumped the grounds, got a fresh filter and fired up a new pot. The hazelnut flavor quickly permeated the tiny house, alerting her senses that she was back in work morning mode.

"Hello coffee and yogurt breakfast. Goodbye cold pizza and booze brunch," Guin muttered to no one.

She buzzed the iron across her shirt, right there on the bare counter, and then held it up. It passed inspection. She poured a cup and attempted to add a little fake cream, but the powder had crystallized into a solid chunk with the recent humidity.

"Screw it." She dropped the mess, coffee and all, into the garbage on the way to the bathroom.

Guin washed her face and blotted it dry, studied herself in the mirror. It didn't look like her liquid brunches or late nights had taken much of a toll. Far be it from her to think that the obligatory time off could have done her any good. But admittedly, she looked rested.

She turned sideways and was pleased with her reflection. In boy briefs and a tank it was easy to appreciate her toned abs and arms. Her long blond hair fell carelessly into near-ringlets complementing her subtle feminine curves. The whole package conspired to confuse men and delight women.

Before, three years ago, she'd been a P.E. coach, and her long, lean musculature still proved it. The teenage angst-ridden air had squeezed the life out of her. She was too inclined to become entangled in their issues, a casualty of working with high schoolers. At least she knew that about herself.

And she knew how to use her gifts. All of them.

She was well aware that her green eyes caused admirers to get a little congested in the brain space; they were the voodoo that made people forget about her kick-ass side, which in turn was what made her such a great cop. Those eyes were as much a weapon as her gun, as much a part of her power as her psychic gift. It seemed almost unfair to deliver such a sucker punch to the unsuspecting. And those who did see it coming didn't seem to mind much.

As for her personal life, it was never a problem finding someone soft to cozy up with on a chilly night. Or any night, for that matter.

She pulled her shirt on, squeezed a line of Crest on her toothbrush. She tried not to focus too much on the day ahead, or the reason for her spontaneous vacation in the first place. They could give her all the time in the world and it wouldn't erase her crystal clear memory of that day. Now everybody would have their eyes trained on her. It was just human nature.

Guin buttoned her shirt, all the while staring into her own eyes as if she, too, were anxious to see what she would do. She grabbed her belt off the doorknob, looped it through and started to buckle it when it happened. She gasped and released it, as if it were made of fire. The memory of Cheryl unbuckling it only a month earlier hit her like a punch in the gut.

Guin sighed so deeply she wondered if she might deflate right on the spot. She angrily shook her head, blond curls bobbing wildly as she grabbed the buckle anyway and fastened it.

"You'll have to stop that," she warned herself. There was sure to be a lot more "memory" at the office, encrypted everywhere, waiting for her to revisit it.

She'd once tried to explain this touch-thing to Terence, the closest person to a brother she had. He was her former colleague. They'd worked together before he'd transferred divisions to become a CSI. Terence was gay, and he too had blond hair and green eyes. They joked that they could actually have shared a womb. When Terence had given her a funny look about her revelation, she set out to prove her ability.

"Just give me anything out of your closet and I'll tell you what you were doing the last time you wore it." She held out her hand.

"Okay..." Terence found a random sweater and held it up. "Here you go. Amaze me."

"Orange?" She made a rather judgmental smirk.

Terence folded his arms, the sweater still clenched in his hand. "What's wrong with orange?"

"Nothing," she quietly answered, then added under her breath, "if you're a pumpkin."

"Whatever, Guin. When I had my colors done I was told I was an autumn." Then when she still stared at him, he shook his head. "Just because you don't understand color coordination, doesn't mean—"

She held her hand up to halt his queen-rant. "Please, stop right there, Oleg. I have a hard enough time making sure my socks match on a good day." She made a gimme motion. "Now fork over the sweater."

Feigning insult, he handed it to her.

"Let's get this over with. And it better not be X-rated." She closed her eyes, heard Prince's "Little Red Corvette," saw Terence skating with his handsome friend. A large banner read, Gay Skate, Valentine's Day, 2007.

She made her concise summary and held up the orange garment with a twitchy little smile. He didn't take it right away.

"What? You don't believe me?" She waved the sweater at him. "You think it was sewn in the collar or something?"

Terence flipped back the tag for a peek.

"You're kidding me. Tell me you don't scrapbook your sweaters."

He removed his hand, folded his arms like an indignant child. "Lucky guess."

Guin laughed in disbelief. "Lucky guess?" She sighed with disgust, clutched the sweater back to her chest, and closed her eyes again.

In her vision, Terence skated to a wall. Guin narrated the years-ago conversation.

"Wow, this is more exhausting than I remember. And I don't seem to remember that song being that long." She snapped her eyelids open and pointed at Terence, and added, "Which was 'Little Red Corvette' by the way." She shut her eyes again, continued narrating what she heard in her vision. "All I could think about was how much I wanted it to end so that I could stop and do this..." Guin's eyelids snapped open again. She grimaced. "Jesus, you guys were cornballs. But he was a cutie, I'll say that much."

Terence, past the point of believing her touch-induced vision was merely a parlor trick, quietly stood there, mouth gaping, eyes wide.

"Here, take the sweater." She tried to hand it back. "Come on, it's no big deal. Who was he?"

"Jack," he finally managed to say. He shook his head, blinked. "How...?"

Guin shrugged. "Just happens. Did I ever meet Jack?"

"He was a one-time thing during an off-again phase with Tony." Terence lapsed into a brief reverie, as if momentarily forgetting what had just happened. But his smile quickly evaporated and he stared at her. "You saw that?"

"Yeah, dude. That's what I've been trying to tell you." She wriggled her eyebrows playfully, shoved the sweater at him one last time. "Pretty crazy, huh?"

Terence tossed it aside, looked around. "Let's try something else."

"More proof? You don't believe me?" She laughed. "Like I'm some kind of circus freak show or something..."

"No, it's not that." But he didn't sound terribly convincing. He walked around the room snatching up odds and ends before returning to stand before her.

Guin shook her head, started to refuse, but saw the wounded puppy look in her friend's eyes. She rolled her own eyes and held out her hand for the first item, muttering, "It's like having an all-access pass to the nut farm, huh?"

"It's not nutty or freaky. It's cool." He handed her a watch.

"From...an older woman. Family resemblance—probably Grandma. Oh, you look so cute in your cap and gown." She gave the rote description, then added, "And no, it's not inscribed on the back."

Terence snatched it away, grimaced, but hurriedly replaced it with a book.

"From a hot guy—French? You two had a thing. Why didn't you go on that six-month sabbatical with him?" She tipped her head to the side. "Humph, a naughty professor."

"Oui oui! Unbelievable!" He laughed, snatched it away, and quickly replaced it with a jacket.

"From Bode, who you never mentioned before, you were both lifeguards. You still wear it when you get sentimental and long for your youth. You wore it yesterday, even. To the gym. You ran home in it afterward."

Terence covered his O-shaped mouth with both hands and stifled the highest pitched laugh ever. "You knew all that from this jacket! Holy shit!"

Guin opened her eyes, pinched the garment between her

fingers, and handed it back with a grimace. "I have other senses too, like the sense of smell. Jesus, do you ever wash that thing?"

When he didn't take it she dropped it on top of the same heap where he'd tossed the other things. He clapped his hands with glee, turned a queenly half-circle, then got whisper-like. "Do you know what you could do with this? You could make a fortune! Books! Your own TV show! Appearances!"

"Do you think I like this shit, Terence?" From his face, her turn toward seriousness caused his cloud to plummet. "I've had to live with fragments of this gift since I was born. It comes and goes as it pleases. I gotta tell you, I'd rather not."

She was confounded by this alleged "calling"—at least that's what Granny June called it. As far as Guin was concerned, it was more of a curse in a constant state of flux.

Terence had never called upon her abilities in the name of entertainment again. Instead, he'd found another use for it, but utilized her power sparingly, when there was no other way. Like the time the Morgan kid went missing. He was grateful for her clarity, but hated like hell what she had to say when he'd handed her that tiny shoe. He'd never looked at seemingly perfect parents the same way again.

Guin checked the mirror, straightened her collar, her pins, checked her badge, secured her gunless holster—she'd get her gun back today—all the while noticing the bewildered look in her own eyes. Granny June's sweet, concerned face flashed through her mind. Her face, before the call that fateful day. She blinked it away.

"Let's do this," she said with less enthusiasm than she would have liked. She punched sweats into her gym bag, headed out and locked up. She jogged down the front steps and considered the day ahead of her with little relish. Day one back on the job.

One month changes a girl.

One month ago Guin had been buzzing along in her reasonably happy, rather co-dependent, probably could-stand-therapy sort of life. Then came the call.

It really was the minute that changed...everything.

CHAPTER TWO

One month and six days earlier...

The doorknob was a conglomeration of guilt and lies.

Guin drew her hand back, blinked a few times as she stood on the front porch of her tiny house.

Beth was already there. She'd entered the home an hour earlier, fresh from some highfalutin, lawyerly meeting, and was impatiently waiting for Guin to arrive home.

An onslaught of visions flooded Guin's brain—dinner, her feigning interest in Beth's self-important legal-jargon one-way chatter, blah, blah, blah, and then mind-blowing sex. The doorknob only told the story of Beth's arrival. Guin knew the rest by heart—no supernatural skills needed there. It was always the same thing.

She gingerly rested her hand on the knob again, reveled in the dark feeling there. She wished more than anything that she'd thought to bring her gloves along. Now she was making an unnecessary trip home, which would involve an unnecessary confrontation.

There was a secret side to Beth that both scared and delighted Guin, and sadly would inevitably reveal itself. She would have preferred to spend her days—and more importantly, her nights—basking in this obscure shadow. If only everything didn't have a story to tell her. It really left very little mystery about her women, often painted them evil, downright shallow. A supreme disappointment. She sighed.

"Shit," she muttered, clutching the doorknob firmly. She gave it a turn before she changed her mind. It was her house, after all. Guin stepped inside and counted to three.

By two, Beth was in the living room.

"There you are. I wondered if you moved out." Ruby red lips, pale skin, opulent dark tresses...Guin's smile twitched as she studied her almost-girlfriend from across the room.

Beth was the kind of slender that was achieved less through hard work and more through hard cash. Her plumped lips and high cheekbones hinted that she had a surgeon on retainer. She was statuesque in her three-inch heel Manolos, and her all-black designer suit dress made the announcement to West Coast hippies that she was authentic New York. Indeed.

Her crisp white blouse was unbuttoned enough to offer the tiniest peek behind the scenes—voluptuous breasts brimming the tops of La Perla demi-cups. Jesus. Guin swallowed hard, clenched her eyes shut for a second, dizzy with an overriding instinct to drop her gym bag and remove every last drop of that expensive lace with her teeth.

Beth dipped her head, looked troubled. "What's wrong with you?"

In an odd synchronization, she took a step toward Guin as Guin took a step backward. The front door was squarely behind her. She tightened her grip on her bag strap.

"Nothing, sorry." Guin blinked, cleared her throat. "I'm going to the gym."

Guin dodged Beth's look, went to the chair and grabbed her gloves.

"But you just got here," Beth said, aggravation in her voice. She turned on a different tactic, one that almost always worked. Lowered her eyes, batted her jet black lashes, pursed her full, red lips. "We're going out to a nice romantic dinner, remember?" Then she added in her sultry voice, "And I'm dessert."

Guin's smile twitched. "Sounds delicious. I can't wait to get home."

Beth's mood darkened quickly. "Didn't you already work out once today?"

Guin stopped directly in front of her. "Baby, it was a long day at work. God, we had this ten-thirty-eight that—"

"I've had a long day, too." Beth cut her off, void of any sympathy. "Depositions, a preliminary hearing..." She stopped short when she realized her words were floating right past Guin's ears. She sighed, softened her mood. "Besides, I had a different kind of workout in mind."

She leaned into Guin, kissed her softly, then more deeply. When she drew back, Guin's eyes were still closed. A small smile played on her lips.

"That's nice."

"It is, isn't it?" Beth purred.

"Very." Guin nodded, whispered, "And as soon as I get back we'll eat out."

Beth raised the stakes, whispered seductively, "What if I don't feel like dinner?"

"Who said anything about food?" Guin chuckled softly. "I'll hurry."

Beth's tone turned again. It was hard to keep up. "But I'm leaving tomorrow, Guin. Won't you miss me?"

Guin's eyelids sprang open and she contemplated calling a penalty. Would she miss her? Something felt different. Wrong. For as long as Guin could remember, physical exercise had been her only means of slaying this strange, occasional demon. She held steadfast to her guns. "I'll be back in an hour, promise."

"Guin, you know my schedule exactly. I'm here for three days, New York for four." She thrust her hands on her tiny hips, stared Guin down. "Is it asking too much to spend the few days I have here with you?"

Guin's shoulders rounded slightly. She breathed a heavy sigh. "I'm not going to argue with you during the little bit of time we have together."

"Little bit of time is right. Whose fault is that?" Beth asked. "It's not like I'm asking for a commitment here."

Guin blinked, felt her lips twitch. "Really?"

They stared at each other for several seconds. The remainder of Beth's cool demeanor vanished, replaced by a look so cold, it chilled the entire room.

"Fine," she said curtly.

Guin knew she should say something reassuring. This stuff always got her into trouble. But she knew herself, knew her needs, and knew she had to make a speedy exit before the sickening unidentifiable feeling swallowed her whole. She backed away, felt her heartbeat quicken. Freedom beckoned her from the other side of the door.

"Wait." Beth strode across the room with a laundry bag looped around her perfectly manicured fingertip. With near contempt, she practically tossed it at Guin. "Drop this at the dry cleaner, won't you?" Her request sounded more like maid's orders.

Guin caught the bag against her chest. As soon as she touched it, a vision came to her so clear it was practically high definition. It was Beth, curled up with a pretty, early-twenties woman, presumably Jenn, her New York lover, in the high-backed booth of an unidentifiable restaurant. She saw their mutual admiration, heard their sweet exchange.

"I hate it when you're gone," Jenn whispered.

"I know, baby."

"I've been saving this to tell you in person. I got some good news from the doctor today." Jenn touched her nonexistent belly. "It took. Beth, we're going to be mommies."

Beth's face lit up. She scooted as close as possible to Jenn, kissed her over and over...

Guin snapped back to present, dropped the bag and stared down at it.

"Be careful, that's a good suit," Beth scolded her.

Guin picked it up, regarded it like poison. In a way, it was. Her stomach churned. That deep, dark feeling...

"Does...Jenn take care of this for you when you're in New York?" Guin quietly delivered the blow and watched Beth's eyes angrily flare, then harden again. Confirmation. They remained quietly staring at each other until Guin shrugged, muttered, "Just curious."

The gym was practically empty, the only sound the dull thud-thudding of Guin's gloves against the bag. She went at it until she'd killed every last lie, then slumped exhausted onto the mat. She shook off one glove, spun the lid on her water bottle and slugged it down. She glanced at the wall clock and realized she'd been there for two hours. As depleted as she felt, she had it pegged to be at least four. She could have worked out her frustration all night, but Barney, the receptionist, was waiting to close up shop. Still, what to do with Beth?

Her cell buzzed and vibrated across the mat. Guin shook off her other glove and chased it. She'd ignored it two other times during her frenzy. It was Beth, of course, and probably mad as hell that she was late. She ignored it this time, too, gathered her stuff and went to shower.

On the way to her car, she decided it was time to face the music. She hit the callback button. It rang only once. She mustered some enthusiasm. "Hey, I saw I missed your call, sorry."

"Just wanted to let you know that I'm taking an earlier flight back to New York," Beth informed her. No hello. Nothing.

"Tonight? Uh, okay." Guin threw her bag in the backseat, got in and started her car. "I'll take you to the airport. We'll grab a bite on the way."

"Not necessary. I've already called a cab."

"Okay," Guin slowly answered. "What about your suits? You need them? I had them put a rush on for pickup tomorrow morning."

"No worries. I've got plenty to choose from."

Women or suits? Guin wondered. She shook her head. "Yeah,

I know you do." She waited a beat, felt compelled to add, "So, I'll see you in a few days, then?"

"Sure. Goodbye, Guin."

Guin had to check the screen to see if the call had actually ended. It had.

"Whatever," she muttered, and tossed the phone onto the passenger seat. Funny, despite it all, she'd actually been looking forward to spending time with Beth. Or spending time with someone, anyway. Her capacity to relate to other women—in an actual, bona-fide relationship—was surprisingly shallow. Too many secrets. Well, one anyway. And she wasn't about to share that with any woman she dated. Hell, it only takes three to sign committal paperwork. Guin laughed at her predicament, rubbed her forehead.

If she was going to share her secret with anyone, it would be someone she trusted implicitly. Someone she truly felt at peace with. That would be Cheryl.

She put the car in park, left it running at the exit of the empty parking lot. Then Guin rummaged around, suddenly desperate to find anything Cheryl had touched, work-related or not. Just something that—if only for a moment—would let Guin feel the undeniable sensation of affection she felt whenever she was with her partner.

She checked her bag, swiped her hand through the console compartment, between the seats and along the floor. Not even a damned dime had slipped out of Cheryl's pocket. Guin had had their winter patrol jackets in the trunk for cleaning, but had dropped them off hours ago when she'd taken Beth's fancy suits to the dry cleaner, on a separate ticket of course.

Guin was accustomed to having women "accidentally" leave things behind—lipstick in the car, socks in her dryer, hairdryer in her bathroom—subtle reminders they'd been there. Or perhaps it was territory claiming, an attempt at relaying to anyone who might come after them that Guin had belonged to someone.

But Guin had never belonged to anyone, really. The only one with whom she would consider such an arrangement was firmly ensconced in a different arrangement.

Cheryl didn't leave behind a drop of evidence that she'd ever been there. Was it the detail-oriented cop in her, or the mother? Guin contemplated this as she snatched up her phone and stared at it. With some reluctance, she punched a single number. Yeah, Cheryl had managed to rate speed dial.

"Hello?" Cheryl sounded breathless when she picked up. Her tone brightened significantly when she heard her lover's voice. "Hey, you. How are you?"

"I'm good." Guin practically smiled out loud. Sweet relief. She could easily imagine Cheryl with her dark hair pulled loosely away from her face, a few straying bangs beautifully framing her eyes...wearing her sweat capris—or "mom pants" as Guin would joking call them. In her lopsided shirt and bare feet, she was beautiful.

She could hear Cheryl's scooting across hardwood floors as she raced through the house on a mission of toy collection that her sons, Frankie and Michael, had scattered everywhere. Guin knew the routine and smiled when she thought about the boys. Then there was Frank, who would be home soon for an hour-long dinner, and then back he'd go to the office for the evening. Frank being Cheryl's husband, things were...complicated.

"It's nice to hear your voice."

"Yours too. Look, I was wondering if you had a little time to yourself later. Thought you might drop the kids by your mom's."

"Sweetie, I wish I did." There was no mistaking the genuine regret in Cheryl's voice. In fact, there was no mistaking anything about the woman at all. It was refreshing—something Guin had never experienced before. Jesus, surely she wasn't in love... "Frank's taking off early tonight. He'll be home in a few minutes for dinner, which I haven't even considered yet."

She heard Cheryl rifling through cabinets.

"How about Tuna Helper."

"Funny girl," Cheryl remarked. "What's wrong, sweetie? I thought you had a night planned with Beth?"

"She went back to New York early. Again." This happened a lot.

"I see." The noises stopped. Cheryl sighed and gave Guin

her full attention. "I'm sorry, hon. And you know how much I hate saying no to you."

Guin did know. She heard the sound of a door opening in the background.

"Hon, I've got to go. Frank just got home." Her voice dropped to a near whisper. "I'll see what his schedule is for the rest of the week. No need for you to sit home all by your lonesome."

Guin smiled half-heartedly. "Well, you do know how lonely I get."

"Do I ever. I've got to go."

It would have been an extreme letdown had Guin not recognized the same heartache in Cheryl's voice. Sometimes you just know when it's right with someone. And sometimes that someone has a husband and two kids in grade school. She rubbed her forehead, sighed deeply. It would be an especially lonely night.

Guin drifted off momentarily. Maybe she'd tell Cheryl. And what would she tell her, exactly? That she was a psychic? A visionary? Jesus, if only she could get a grip on this damned power of hers to do something useful—like read minds in real-time. Then she'd know if Cheryl would ever actually consider leaving Frank for her...

Guin shook her head as if she could physically make the thought go away. She didn't need to torture herself for no reason, especially when girls like Beth were waiting on the sidelines to take a swipe. She knew Cheryl would never do that to her.

"Oh boy," she lamented to no one.

Guin looked for her phone, which had fallen onto the floor mat. God knows how long she'd been sitting at that parking lot stop sign. She didn't even need touch to induce visions of Cheryl anymore. They were etched in her mind, and on her heart.

Her hands felt shaky and a lump had formed in her throat. She pulled out of the parking lot, but instead of heading for the freeway, pulled straight into a different lot. Guin got out, clicked her car locks and headed for a dingy tavern she knew well that did not know her back. She came here alone, never brought so much as a friend. It was her secret—possibly the single place with no personal residual memories. And thankfully, it appeared to be as empty as the gym had been.

She quickly took a stool, ordered a drink and stared at her trembling hands while she waited. She slowly turned them over and pressed her palms flat against the dilapidated bar with hearts and initials carved into it. She waited to feel something. In a moment she'd have a stomach full of warm tequila and a head full of heartaches and regrets that were not her own. It was a sick way to achieve any measure of comfort at all.

CHAPTER THREE

The steeply winding trail was really no match for her that day. Only two miles into the hike, Guin noticed she'd lost her running partner. She hit a plateau and paused to let him catch up, struck a yoga pose, twisted right, then left.

It was a spectacular day for a much needed therapeutic run; tepid weather, relatively quiet in these parts of the Hollywood Hills near the reservoir. She lunged into a slow squat, felt every ounce of the burn, turned to the other side.

"What the hell...?" Terence closed a sizeable gap in their paces, dragging up the trail. Sweat had formed up the center of his shirt like a widening spine, seeping out to greet his armpits in a sweaty T. Breathing hard, he reached down and brushed the red dust off his clean Nikes. "Hello? Did I know we were racing? What are you—training for a marathon?"

"Sorry, I've got a lot on my mind today." She shook her arms out, wrapped one around her opposite shoulder and leaned into it for a good stretch. "It's beautiful out here, huh?"

Terence bent at the waist as if he would puke. He rested the heels of his hands on his thighs. He closed his eyes. "Yeah, I love it here." Then he spat out his correction, "Well, I love it here when I'm not running with you."

"I'll try to go easier on you." Guin's lips twitched into a little smile. She gazed around the vast openness. The Hollywood sign was visible up ahead, a quiet residential area just below. "I've always thought this was a groovy neighborhood. Big money, old names."

"Très Hollywood, baby." Terence stood, spiraled his index finger in the air, as if deciding where he wanted his pointer to land. He aimed it at a faded pink and yellow wall a good distance ahead of them. "There, Madonna's old estate. To your far right and back a few, it's Britney's post K-Fed crash-pad. Kevin Costner has a lovely Spanish style around the block there, and Denzel's layout only a few houses down. Paradise."

"Stalk much? Shall I put Kevin and Denzel on alert?" She smiled at her best friend. She had a feeling his information was far more reliable than any Map of the Stars. He looked offended. She raised her hands defensively. "It's a little creepy, that's all I'm saying."

He surveyed the steep grade, the houses, the well-worn trails and beautiful homes. "Yeah, if it wasn't for an occasional dead body rolling down the canyon, this place would be almost perfect."

"I got called to one of those," they said in unison, grinned, and then, "Me too." The pair pointed at each other. "Jinx."

She dropped into a right lunge and looked ready to go again.

"Seriously though, what's on your mind?" Terence stretched his back. He was obviously in no hurry. "This Beth thing? Again?"

Guin shot him a look. "Yeah, well. I like her, it's just that she's a little—"

"Bitchy?" he assisted. "High maintenance? Prima donna? Sociopathic…?"

"Whoa, Tex. Hold up." She couldn't help but softly chuckle. "She is some of those things."

"Some?" Terence's eyes were wide as saucers. "Understatement of the year."

Guin pursed her lips, didn't disagree. She turned thoughtful. "Then there's Cheryl."

"Married Cheryl. Yes, I know the one." He nodded eagerly, pointedly ignoring the look Guin gave him. He turned on his best storytelling narrative. "Married Cheryl, with a husband, and little children, and a house, probably a family pet...correct?"

Guin openly stared him down.

He stepped up behind her, touched the small of her back, spoke confidentially as other hikers passed by them. "If you ask me, it seems like we're developing a little pattern here."

"I don't recall asking you." Guin broke away, snatched up a few rocks, tossed them into the reservoir.

He ignored her remark, continued his lecture. "Guin, all the women you date are not available. Except for sex."

She wanted to tell him he was wrong. "Yeah, well. That way I don't have to get too involved."

Terence shook his head. "That's what your head says, but your heart seems to be having a little trouble dealing with that theory. If you ask me."

"And again, I did not." She sighed, felt tension in her neck, rolled her head from side to side. "I just haven't found the right person yet. You know, someone I can share everything with."

"Ah, you mean..." Terence twinkled his fingers. "The Guin magic."

"Stop with the jazz hands." She focused on the water, didn't want him trying to read her mind. Surprisingly, he was getting rather good at it. Jesus, she couldn't afford to be so transparent. "Yeah, the...magic." She shrugged. "It's not something I'm exactly comfortable bringing up. People would think I'm a freak."

She recalled as a little girl trying to tell a grade school teacher about it. She'd been promptly hauled off to the counselor's office and then her mom was summoned into the mix. The school's administrators expressed "extreme concern" which caused her mother to blow up. Not because she gave a shit about her kid, but because more than likely they'd interrupted happy hour. Consequently, it was the first of many times Guin switched schools. It was a tough lesson. She didn't mention her power for the balance of her school career.

But kids had known back then that she was different. Thankfully they weren't able to define precisely what that difference was. She was simply labeled weird. A freak. If only they really knew how much. Even so, their torture was relentless, and accounted for the second and third times she'd switched schools in her childhood. Thank God for open enrollment.

She imagined that telling anyone today might yield a similar outcome. Too risky, most especially for a cop.

"Yeah," she quietly said on the tail end of the haunting flashback. "Definitely they would think I'm a freak."

"In this town?" He elbowed her playfully. "You're in Hollyweird, baby."

"Well, then I guess I fit right in."

"Look, everything will fall into place. I don't have to be a psychic to know that."

She looked at him. He was serious. "You think?"

"Cheer up. You'll meet someone who won't have a problem with you being one of the chosen ones." He playfully hooked air quotes.

Guin didn't buy it. "That sounds nice, Terence. But I really don't think that's going to happen." She gazed up at the skies, as if she could physically address the spirit or whatever power was responsible for assigning her the special gift. "You could very well have chosen the wrong one! Do you hear me? Are you listening up there?"

Terence looked around them at other hikers who hadn't seemed to notice her odd performance. Still, he quieted her. "Okay, let's take it down a notch. Hello, drama."

"Yeah, I'd hate for them to think I'm crazy." Guin shook her head, her eyes turning slightly misty.

He patted her back. "Honey, you're still just learnin' all the tricks. That's all."

Guin toughened up, refused to be a baby. She nodded. "Yeah. It's not like this...this superpower came with a manual."

"No. But girl, you would look fabulous in the cape," he whispered.

It was comfort that only Terence could administer. She smiled at last, covered her lips slightly so he wouldn't know how good a job he'd done cheering her.

"Let's walk." He grabbed her arm as if to keep her from sprinting off. They started back on the path. "You know, if I had your powers, I'd definitely use them for good, if you know what I mean." He nodded, wriggled his eyebrows playfully. "And I think you do."

Guin grinned at him. "You're nutty. Come on." She took a few steps, preparing to launch into a sprint.

"Oh, Christ…"

"Yeah, you're going to need superpowers to keep up…" She literally left him in the dust.

Guin waited for him at her car for nearly ten minutes. Then Terence, looking wiped out, showed at last. He practically dragged himself to the parking lot. She ignored his death glare, handed him a water bottle. "Chin up, little buckaroo. Next up, lunch. My treat."

"As if I could eat after that." He took a long swig of water, swiped the sweat off his forehead. "Your self-loathing is killing me."

They watched as a lesbian couple got out of their Jeep with a floppy Labrador puppy in tow. They leashed the pet, casually grabbed hands, and started up the hill toward the dog park.

"I want that," Guin said softly.

"Tell me you're talking about the puppy." They watched the pair until they were out of sight. Terence shook his head, softened. "Trust me, you do not want to get into a new relationship in your present needy state of mind. That's just inviting in more crazy." He shot her a look. "No offense. And remember that even without the problem of your special gift, relationships aren't all they're cracked up to be."

"Maybe not. But just one time, I'd like to hold someone without knowing all the bad shit they've done behind my back. Lay down in a bed without knowing who snuck out of it that morning—that kind of thing." She shrugged. "It's not easy is all I'm saying."

"Oh, sweetie." Terence went to hug her, but she cringed and took a step back.

"Thanks anyway, sweaty boy."

Terence looked thoughtful. "Guin, listen to what you're saying. The problem isn't your special powers. It's a case of you repeatedly picking the wrong women."

She rolled her eyes.

"Why do you think you're getting all that bad mojo off them? You know, you get in these moods, see things like that—" He waved toward the path where the happy couple had been moments earlier "—and you get all sentimental, all sad, all... needy. And then you grab the first woman who smiles your way."

"A lot of women smile my way, Terence," she said with a touch of resentment.

She started to get in the car, but Terence caught her shoulder, kept her attention. "If you're serious about wanting a real relationship, you need to decide what is most important to you. Make a list and don't stop until you've found someone with all those qualities."

"Just like that," she said, her disbelief clear in her voice. "A list."

"Ask the universe and you shall receive." He sounded like Dr. Phil. "Get as picky as you want. Don't settle for another Monica. Or Lynn." He appeared to consider it. "Or Trinity. Or Beth. Or...what was the girl's name...? The one with the funky piercing in her—"

"I get what you're saying." She leaned against the car, toed the gravel with her running shoe. "What if I've already found her?"

"Hello? Was 'married woman' on your list?" He dramatically threw his hands on his hips when she shrugged. Then he wagged his index finger in her face. "I think no."

"I think I'm going to tell Cheryl," Guin announced.

"I think that's a mistake."

"I don't think I'll lose her."

Terence leaned away from the car slightly, gauged her expression. "Do I need to point out the absurdity of that statement?"

He didn't. Terence dropped back against the car and they quietly watched more dog park patrons unload a variety of canines and head uphill. There were some couples and several lovely singles.

A girly-girl wearing impractical heels and carrying a poodle jumped out of a posh convertible and started toward the path. Her doting boyfriend, purse in hand, was hot on her heels.

Terence broke the silence. "Maybe you should get yourself a dog. They're loyal and loving. No second-guessing involved."

Girly-girl noticed Guin leaning against her car, shot her a wink and blew her a kiss. A crooked smile came to Guin's lips. "Oh, I don't know, Terence. I enjoy a good second-guess."

CHAPTER FOUR

Guin stood before her bedroom mirror strapping on her gun belt. She knew the action by heart—hardly needed a mirror—but used it to study the woman behind her.

Cheryl's natural auburn hair tumbled over bare milky shoulders as she bent to retrieve her uniform. In their frenzy it had become part of a combined heap of blues lying next to Guin's bed. Lunch hour, as it turned out, served to satisfy an entirely different appetite.

Cheryl fished a shirt out of the heap, shook it out and draped it over her camisole.

"Beautiful..." Guin mumbled as she fastened her buckle.

Cheryl stopped mid-shake. She heard it. "I'm sorry?"

Guin looked embarrassed, surprised that the end part of her thought had wafted out of her muddled head. Her cheeks flushed slightly.

"You are beautiful."

Cheryl, wearing only her shirt over a camisole and panties, dropped everything she'd gathered up. Smiling sweetly she approached Guin, wrapped her arms around her waist. She kissed her, leaned toward her ear. "You're pretty beautiful yourself."

"No," Guin quickly protested. She started to pull away, but Cheryl only tightened her embrace.

"You're not good with receiving compliments. I've noticed that about you."

Guin arched an eyebrow. "Yeah, not really."

"You can trust me. Trust my words," Cheryl quietly assured her. "Don't be afraid."

"I'm not." But then Guin amended her words with the quivering statement. "Not much."

It was the closest thing to an admission of vulnerability she'd uttered in years. Cheryl seemed to know this. Guin knew that she too read people well; it was organic, not psychic. It was a major contributing factor that made her a good supervisor.

Cheryl straightened Guin's collar, let her fingers rove down her crisp shirt to the belt buckle. She made a show of slowly buckling it.

"Thank you, Sergeant."

"No problem, Marcus," Cheryl played along. "I wouldn't want you to misrepresent the department by not looking your best."

Guin moved in close. "Really?"

They kissed again.

"Frank's pulling another all-nighter tomorrow night," Cheryl whispered between kisses.

A crooked smile tugged at Guin's lips. "Is that an invitation?"

"Invitation? Hmm..." She looked thoughtful. "I'd say it's more like an order."

"Well, I certainly wouldn't want to be insubordinate."

Cheryl lowered her eyes. "You know I wouldn't tolerate that."

Guin kissed a trail past her collar, headed downward.

"Guin..." Cheryl whispered. "Why don't you have anything on your walls?"

Guin raised up, saw she was serious. "Is there something wrong with that?" she stammered.

"I suppose not." Cheryl was inventorying the room and Guin followed her gaze: dresser, mirror, bed, whitewashed walls, not even a rug. It was perfunctory at best. "Are you some kind of minimalist?"

Guin smiled, looked away. There were so many reasons she lived the way she did. Every picture, every postcard—everything triggered a vision or feeling. It was enough that she dealt with so much in the line of duty. The last thing she wanted was more uninvited stimulus from the single place she trusted to be her solace. It would never be easy to explain to anyone she chose to tell. "You know me better than that."

Cheryl seemed to consider her vague answer then whispered, "I do know you." She kissed her. "I know you very, very well."

The words sent a chill through Guin. She closed her eyes, basked in the bit of security that had been extended to her and wished more than anything she could fully submerge herself in it and forget everything else.

They kissed deeply, their passion escalating once again. Guin ran her hands up her partner's loosely hanging shirt, cupped her breast, felt heat all over again.

"We're not very good at this," Cheryl said, an air of hopelessness in her tone.

"You kidding? We're great at this."

"Not this part," Cheryl said between kisses, smiling, almost laughing. "The part where we try to get dressed."

"No, we're very, very bad at that." Guin's voice dropped to a whisper, "Do you want me to fuck you again?"

Cheryl nearly melted against Guin, nodded quickly. "And then again."

"I don't know…you think you can handle it?" A flick of her belt buckle and the gun belt was around her ankles. Pants came down on top of it. Guin went to work on the buttons of Cheryl's shirt and tossed it onto the heap of clothes along with her camisole. She leaned into Cheryl, couldn't get close enough.

"Why do we get dressed at all?" Cheryl softly laughed.

"Foreplay," Guin answered, smiling. Never breaking

contact, she kissed a sliding path to Cheryl's belly. Then lower. She made love to her with her mouth, touching and teasing her until Cheryl's legs went limp with desire. Cheryl stroked Guin's head.

"Cheryl..." Guin almost choked. Her heart had nearly engaged her mouth without first cycling through her brain. She felt her chest lurch, her stomach didn't feel much better. A mistake like that could cost a girl... She reprocessed whatever intended flowery sentiment she'd nearly fatally uttered, selected a more benign statement. "I am nutty about you."

Cheryl's lips turned up into a small, knowing smile. Guin's insides hopelessly sank.

Cheryl held out her hand and quietly ordered, "Take me to your bed."

They dropped onto the sheets for the preliminaries leading to round two. This time Guin's visions were not touch-induced, but wound through her brain, threatening to strangle every thought of making love to the woman in her bed. Cheryl had a husband, two children, and the thought of those beautiful boys was enough to inspire Guin to order the woman right out of her house. And it wasn't like she didn't have options. Women—particularly well-to-do women, for some reason, threw themselves at her on a regular basis. She had no business getting wrapped up in a woman with so much baggage.

Only it didn't feel like baggage. Guin felt genuine affection for Frankie and Michael. Hell, she even liked husband Frank—how sick was that? An admittedly insane thought tickled the back of her love-weary brain that Frank would somehow fit into this picture; a pool boy, a handyman, a next-door neighbor over for coffee...? As if Frank wouldn't majorly kick her ass if he knew she was fucking his wife.

These odd delusions would not abate. Guin with Cheryl and their happy household of children, a dog, possibly a guinea pig—a school project. Homework, chores, fixing the dishwasher... She couldn't wake from the twisted, iron-clad, happily-ever-after fantasy no matter what light of reason she tried to throw in her own path. Foreign dreams of sublime happiness and normalcy threatened to chip away at her miserable existence.

Fuck it all. She closed her eyes and spun. Sweet orgasm. Guin lay utterly paralyzed.

Breathless, Cheryl nibbled her neck, worked her way up to Guin's ear, whispered, "So, you ready to catch the bad guys now?"

"Hon," Guin muttered, exhausted, half-laughing at herself. "After that, I'm pretty much ready for anything."

"That's my girl." Cheryl sat up. Sunlight hazily streamed in through the sheer curtains illuminating her glowing skin and soft, supple curves.

"I mean it." Guin's voice was a choked rasp. She swallowed hard, repeated her earlier sentiment. "You are beautiful."

She watched her lover gather her clothes for a second time and head for the bathroom. In moments she heard the shower streams and soon small clouds of perfumed steam mistily floated from the open door.

Guin sighed, pushed her weary body over until she sat on the edge of the bed. She was emotionally and physically wrung out. She caught sight of Cheryl's camisole in the center of the floor and went to pick it up. She regarded it cautiously, held it up against the sunlight. Helpless against herself, Guin clutched the article and drew it close to her chest. She closed her eyes and to her relief, felt only great joy and warmth. She proceeded to bury her face in the silky material, smiled, even laughed. She felt happy. She felt loved.

Guin carried the garment into the bathroom and gently placed it on the pile of uniform blues. She softly tapped the shower door and was pleased when Cheryl pushed it open as an invitation.

Later, on their way to their car, Guin wondered what her landlord thought about all the women who entered and exited her tiny pool house on a regular basis. The thought of it made her smile, an action that didn't go unnoticed by Cheryl.

"What's got you grinning like that?"

Embarrassed, Guin shook her head. "I was thinking that I can't imagine tomorrow's dinner topping today's lunch."

They got in and Cheryl promptly slid over to Guin's side, sexily whispered in her ear, "Let's not forget dessert."

Guin shuddered with delight, almost dizzy at the thought. She started up the patrol car, cleared her throat. "Can I ask you a personal question?"

"I just explored your nether regions for an hour and now you want to get personal?" Cheryl practically giggled. "I think that would be okay, Officer Marcus."

But the look on Guin's face said the conversation was about to take a serious turn.

"Do you and your husband..." Guin stammered, almost didn't ask, but was encouraged by the patience that shone in Cheryl's eyes. "I was just wondering how it's all working with you two these days. Rekindling any...fires of love?"

Cheryl leaned back in her seat, finally said, "It's different with Frank and me than it is between us."

"Obviously." Another nervous chuckle.

"Frank is a good man. He's an excellent father." She selected her words carefully, like she was tiptoeing over a minefield. "But he's not my soul mate. I know that now."

Guin swallowed hard, nodded. She didn't dare ask the obvious question. She didn't think she could sustain that injury no matter which direction the answer went. "I see."

"Or did you mean in bed?" Cheryl looked at her earnestly.

"I meant...everything." There was silence.

"You know how I feel about duty," Cheryl stated. Her voice gathering strength. She was always at her best when she was talking shop. "You sign on for a job, you do it to the best of your ability." Then she softened, admitted, "I have a duty to my marriage."

Kapow. A landmine.

"I see." Guin's heart sank. They rode in silence while she gathered her courage. "What about your duty to yourself? What about your right to be happy?"

Cheryl's voice was a well-rehearsed monotone. "I'm happy with my kids. I wish I had the luxury of making all the other things right too." She paused, lowered her voice. "Because I really would like to make you happy."

"Come here." Guin pulled her into a half hug at the stoplight. Cheryl's response was in truth what she feared it would be. "You do make me happy. I respect that you're doing right by your family."

Cheryl wore remorse painfully well. "You seem to know me so well, Guin. It's remarkable. You never push too hard. You're good with me and my...situation."

"Well, at least I'm good at something."

Still, Cheryl looked troubled. "But when it comes to you, there's something you're holding back from me."

Guin blinked, looked out the window, looked anywhere but at the woman in the seat next to her. "You're married, Cheryl. It's always in the back of my mind no matter how I try to pretend you're not."

"It's more than that," she softly said. "There's a darkness about you that I can't pinpoint."

"Well, we all have our dirty little secrets."

"It's not like that. But I do feel you've been carrying something with you for a very long time." Cheryl's hand snaked across the seat, clasped Guin's. "When you're ready, I'd like you to share it with me."

Guin swallowed hard. For a moment it crossed her mind that she might not be the only one in that squad car with a psychic gift. It was hard to believe Cheryl could sense such things about her. She felt transparent, just as she had many times in her presence. She could almost tell her...

"Unit fifty-four, come in."

The fuzzy sound of dispatch infiltrated the car, dispelling any hopes of sharing her secret with Cheryl. Guin's shoulders caved slightly with her disappointment when Cheryl picked up the call. Domestic disturbance. Super.

Guin punched a button, flipped on the lights, and made a skillful, sharp U-turn amidst thick traffic headed toward the freeway. She should tell Cheryl. She owed it to her. After all, her power was no threat to the woman—it was nearly impossible to get a strong read on Cheryl for some reason. She was so different from anyone else she'd ever dated.

Dated?

It was officially complicated. If she spilled her guts to Cheryl, there was a chance she would think she was outright batty. Maybe she'd want to get as far away from her as possible and that would certainly solve Guin's lovesick problems.

But Cheryl had a good heart and when it came down to it, she was the only one Guin could imagine herself with, even in parceled-out increments. Maybe that would be enough. Maybe it could work if she could manage to reprocess those traditional ideals everyone had about happily ever after. Not like she'd had a real clear bead on normalcy in the first place.

She would tell her tomorrow at dinner.

CHAPTER FIVE

Morning came without apology. Guin's head lightly rung from a few too many tequilas the night before. Her nights away from Cheryl were normally spent this way. A bonus round of multiple crazed voice mails left by Beth the Attorney had Guin craving a simple kind of peace. She knew just where to find it.

Granny June could always be found in her picket-fenced idyllic yard. She had sowed her heart into every petal, her soul into every bloom, and was as much a part of that garden as the dirt she'd lovingly hand-packed all around her new bougainvillea. She lifted her eyes, squinted against the sun and greeted Guin.

"Well, good morning, Officer Marcus."

"Good morning."

Granny June peeled off her gloves, played the same game she

always did whenever Guin would stop by in uniform. "And what can I do for you today?"

Guin's lips twitched into a crooked smile. "I just came by to make sure you aren't growing any controlled substances, ma'am."

"Help me up, child." Granny June extended her frail arm and Guin gently assisted her off her padded garden kneeler. She kissed Guin's cheek and patted her shoulder lovingly. "Oh, my knees are gonna be screaming at me tonight."

Guin swung into business mode, brushed her grandmother's silver hair aside. "I'm more worried about that fall you took yesterday." She lightly brushed her thumb along the small bruise on the old woman's cheek. "How do you feel?"

Granny June removed her garden gloves, flipped them airily for effect, scoffed. "This old woman's body has seen worse than that. I'll be fine. Let's sit."

Guin followed Granny June to the old table and chair set next to the small pool. After settling into the vintage cushion, Granny looked at Guin and grinned.

"Relax child. I'm not going to break." Then she looked more closely at Guin. "What is it? Work or love life?"

Guin felt her cheeks warm, smiled and looked away like a child. "Oh, you know. Both."

"Tell Granny June about it."

But Guin surprised both Granny June and herself by shifting the conversation to a topic Granny June was very familiar with. "My visions have been getting stronger, more frequent. They're getting harder to combat." She looked at her, frustrated.

Granny June leaned across the tiny table, took Guin's hand in hers. Their hands were remarkably similar in bone structure, but the elder Marcus's was age spotted, tanned and scarred from years of clashing with thorns.

"Don't try so hard to combat the images. Let them exist." Granny June nodded. "They happen for a reason. Ignoring them will just make you a frustrated old nag."

Guin's smile was fleeting. "But why do I get so much of the negative stuff? I feel like it's poisoning me."

"You have to take the good with the bad." Granny looked

thoughtful, shrugged her bony shoulders. "It doesn't happen overnight. Took me years to understand it. But have faith, you'll get there."

"What if I don't want to know everything?"

"The Good Spirit shows you exactly what's intended for you to see. There's a reason for everything. You've got a powerful gift, Guin. More powerful than I've ever known anyone to have."

It seemed absurd that Granny June would know so many folks with the "gift," but it did run strong through the women in their family. Guin's own mother used to drunkenly joke that she understood why some animals kill their own offspring. She, for one, loathed her gift, and she didn't care much for Guin as a result of hers, either. On the other hand, Granny June had made the very most of her abilities, honed her talents to an expert level. She considered her gift a blessing. Guin hated to admit that she could better understand her mother's feelings about it than her grandmother's.

"We're supposed to help people," Granny said, patting her hand again. "That's what we're here for."

Guin roughly tousled Granny's curls as she contemplated her words. "I just wish sometimes that I could change the channel, you know?"

"Oh, I do." Granny nodded. "But you'll learn to control it and do wonders with it. Give it time. Right now you're still like…a puppy."

Guin shot her a look, chuckled a little.

"Speaking of puppies…" Granny June stood and slowly made her way to a row of pots lined up outside the potting shed. She pulled out a tennis ball and held it out to Guin. Her granddaughter only stared at her with a bewildered expression.

"Have you taken up tennis, Granny?"

"I found it in the shed while I was cleaning up. Here, take it."

With some reluctance, Guin accepted the ball and immediately closed her eyes. She could clearly see Tosha, her beloved terrier mutt, romping across the yard with the ball in tow, enticing Guin until she would give chase. Sounds of barking and her own childish laughter dissipated when she opened her eyes.

Guin smiled broadly. "I loved that dog." She handed the ball back.

"Keep it. It's yours now." Granny June smiled at her. "Use it to clean up after the bad visions. It works every time."

Guin smiled, squeezed the ball again. She set it in her lap. "Is that how you do it? Change channels?"

"Well, something like that. And I have my gardening." Granny June breathed in deeply, raised her tanned face to bask in the sun. "I feel everything good around me. You will learn to as well, in your own time."

The mention of time had Guin looking at her watch. She stood, kissed her grandmother on the cheek. "Thanks, Granny. I hate to cut this short, but I need to get back to work."

Granny stood and hugged her again, more tightly this time. Then Granny June gasped. Guin pulled back slightly, concerned about the distress in her grandmother's face.

"What is it?"

Granny June placed her hand over her heart, giving Guin a first-class scare. "Granny, what is it? Did you see something?"

"No, darling, it's okay," she said at last, slightly breathless. She patted her chest, smiled bravely.

"I don't feel good about this." Guin wasn't reassured by her recovery performance. "I'm taking you to the doctor."

"No, no, darlin'. I'm strong as an old ox and you know it." When her words served to offer little comfort, Granny tried vehemence. "I said go, now. I'm fine."

Guin inspected her. Granny actually seemed fine. A touch to her forehead and then neck confirmed she wasn't clammy. Her pupils were fine. A mystery. "You'll call me if you need anything? Anything at all, right?"

"Don't worry, I've got the number for your...modular phone."

"My cellular phone, Granny." Guin laughed softly, was somewhat comforted by the notion that her grandmother appeared normal and was back to screwing up the language of modern technology. It gave her confidence to leave her for the afternoon.

"Okay, I'm going. But call me if you need anything or if you're feeling bad."

"Sweetie, I'm fine." Granny June hugged Guin to her. "Guin, honey. I want you to be safe today, you hear?"

Guin backed away, gauged her grandmother's expression. She nodded at last. Her grandmother was always telling her that. "I will, Granny."

In the squad car Guin brushed her hands off and wiped the last crumbs from her frozen burrito off her lap. She took a sip of water and glanced in Cheryl's direction.

"Sorry about the Quickie Mart cuisine," she apologized. "I really wanted to check on my grandmother. She took a good spill yesterday. Banged her face up pretty good."

"No worries, hon." Cheryl was no worse for wear and it showed. She smiled, dusted her lap and chucked the wrappers into a brown sack. Guin watched as her partner dabbed at the corners of her mouth with a napkin then slathered sheer lip tint over them. She rubbed them together, made a kissing face and turned to Guin. "Wanna try it out? It's cotton candy."

Guin almost blushed. "My favorite."

"Is it?"

"It is now."

They kissed and when their lips parted, Cheryl whispered, "Lunch was fine. Dinner will be better."

"Jesus, you're going to kill me, I swear..." Guin chuckled, looked down at her clasped hands. With some reluctance, she started the car and drove out of the convenience store parking lot. "Let's finish this day then, already."

On cue, the radio rattled out a trespassing, possible breaking and entering code. On came the lights, another U-turn, and the women were officially back on duty.

The location they'd been dispatched to wasn't far from their lunch stop. An eerie feeling settled in the middle of Guin's chest, and she wondered if it pertained to something wonderful, like dinner where no one would eat, or if it was something else.

She looked sideways at Cheryl; saw how the sunlight illuminated her features just as it had yesterday in her bedroom. It struck her that Cheryl was too good for this world, too vulnerable. It also occurred to Guin that she was taking advantage of her partner's genuineness. Cheryl had a husband and children. She didn't need someone coming along and wrecking it all.

Guin's throat felt tight. She pulled curbside a few numbers down from their destination, they got out and started toward the driveway. Shouts and screams had them hurriedly rerouting toward the backyard. Both women drew their weapons. Cheryl stood flush against the garage that divided the front and back yards and turned to Guin.

"Call for backup." At the sound of smashing glass Cheryl raised her gun. "I'm going to check that out."

"I'll cover you."

"No. Call for backup," Cheryl ordered.

No matter what they were to each other personally, Cheryl was her superior. She watched her partner slide along the backside of the garage and moved away from her and flipped on her radio.

"Unit fifty-four, on location twenty-nine hundred block of Banner Avenue. Possible four-fifteen, requesting backup."

The dispatcher made the speedy announcement. "Requesting all area units for backup, twenty-nine hundred block of Banner Avenue for a possible four-fifteen. Unit fifty-four on the scene."

Guin hurriedly turned the volume of her radio down, slid alongside the garage on the same route Cheryl had taken, despite her order to stay behind. Only the sound of distant traffic could be heard; everything was still. She crept closer to the edge of the building, but still couldn't see her partner. She spoke softly into her radio. "Sergeant Jones, do you copy?"

There was no answer. Guin dropped her head against the garage wall, sighed.

"Hurry on that backup," she muttered under her breath.

As if it was a premonitory statement, two shots rang out. Guin's eyes went wide. She grabbed her mic, hollered, "Shots fired! Shots fired! Requesting immediate assistance! Where's my backup!"

Guin rounded the corner, still bellowing into her radio. "Sergeant Jones, do you copy?" No answer. She scanned the yard. Then she saw Cheryl lying on the lawn. Motionless.

CHAPTER SIX

"Officer down!" She screamed into her mic. "Do you copy?
Officer down!"

With no regard for her own safety, Guin ran to her, fell to
her knees beside Cheryl, checked her throat for a pulse.

"Cheryl!" She grabbed her collar, picked her up and shook
her—did the anti of everything she'd been instructed to do to a
mortally injured person. "Cheryl!"

Guin ran her hands across Cheryl's blood-soaked shirt, felt
nauseous as she started compressions. Nothing. She proceeded
to mouth to mouth, alternated back to chest compressions in
spastic movements. Again she screamed into her collar mic.
"Goddammit! We need a bus! Can't you hear me? Can't anybody
hear me!"

No response from dispatch. No pulse from her partner. Not a single breath.

"No! No, no, no..." Guin screamed, tears streaming down her face and she pounded Cheryl's chest with clenched fists. She'd lost all control. Blood was everywhere. She crumpled over her partner's lifeless body and openly sobbed. Sirens were too far away. She felt a touch on her shoulder and raised up slightly, still shielding the body.

Cheryl was standing squarely before Guin and...Cheryl.

Guin recognized the ethereal quality of her appearance, had been there before other times with other people...

"No! No Cheryl, please don't go!" She reached out to her. "Stay! Please baby, please don't die. Fight to stay with me!"

Cheryl sweetly smiled. She radiated pure peacefulness.

"No. I can't do that."

"Yes, you can!" Guin spat. She was painfully aware that she was chastising a ghost—all but ordering Cheryl's spirit back into her body! That Cheryl's ghost was there told her it was already too late. She wept uncontrollably. "No! My God...no..."

"He is wearing a black racing shirt with a number twelve on it."

"What...?" The perp was really the last thing on Guin's mind. "No—no! Please, Cheryl!"

"Goodbye, Guin." Cheryl's image began to fade right before her eyes. "I love you. I always have."

"No!" Guin screamed. She lunged for the spirit, but as soon as she broke physical contact with Cheryl's dead body, the spirit vanished, an action as precise as turning off a television. Desperately, Guin fell back onto the body. Nothing. Fury burned in her words. "You get back in here! Right this goddamned minute!"

She felt a hand on her shoulder.

But it was Sergeant Winters from evening shift. He and his brawny partner, Officer Burnette, firmly but kindly coaxed her away from the body as paramedics converged on the scene and swarmed around them. Still sobbing, Guin helplessly stood by and watched their futile efforts, deafened by the sound of helicopters buzzing overhead in their search for the suspect.

She didn't remember being driven back downtown. In Captain Briggs's office, she sat alone for an hour. It didn't matter; she had no place to be. The crystal of Guin's watch was covered in Cheryl's dried blood. She dropped her arm back to her lap. The blood made it impossible for her to even fantasize none of this had happened and she was still meeting Cheryl for dinner. She wondered if Frank had been called. He was probably at the station already. And the boys, Frankie and Michael...

Guin cupped her forehead in her hand, leaned over, felt sick but had nothing left in her stomach. She wanted to weep but had no more tears left in her either.

Captain Briggs entered his office and shut the door behind him, motioned for Guin to remain as she was. In the dim, late afternoon sunlight, he took his seat, clasped his hands in front of him and contemplated her.

"I'm sorry for your loss."

It was an unusual greeting, the sentiment they'd been trained to offer civilians when they'd lost a loved one. Jesus, she hated making those house calls. And now she knew that it felt every bit as weak as it sounded when she'd been forced to say it. Empty words void of true empathy. How could anyone possibly understand?

As Guin blankly stared at him, Briggs suddenly looked more like a friend than her boss as he looked at her blood-soaked uniform. "Christ, I'm sorry. We should have let you get cleaned up."

"Crime lab took pictures," she softly droned, business as usual. She looked down at her socks. "Took my boots."

He nodded. They both knew the drill. Guin fiddled with the band on her hat as it lay in her lap, concentrated on simply breathing.

"Marcus, I don't know what you're feeling, but I'm sorry you're feeling it." He opened his drawer, withdrew a form.

She said, "I hate this day." The childish statement was the best she could conjure up. Briggs nodded understanding. Her shock was still evident, her voice a mere monotone. "Do what you have to do and let's get it over with."

"IA will be involved as with any officer's..." Briggs didn't dare say death, only nodded to indicate. Guin nodded, understood, but hated the hell out of Internal Affairs. Always sending their nosiest weasels around, trying to sniff out bad or incompetent cops. "You don't have anything to worry about, of course. Just protocol."

"I know." She set her hat on the chair next to her, sighed. "You're good at this, all things considered."

He didn't respond; he didn't have to. Guin had tremendous respect for Briggs, as most of the other officers did. He was fair, honest, and at the moment he was also hurting at the loss of a key officer. She appreciated him not proffering up mindless one-liners, like, "I know how you feel." She was fairly sure he knew exactly why he couldn't say that. Guin was grateful that he didn't remark on it.

Guin pretended to scratch something on her cheek, tried to appear focused, calm. She casually examined her fingernails, saw the blood deeply embedded in every crevice of her hand, and dropped it back onto her lap. No, there was no fooling herself out of just how very bad a day it had been. A lump formed in her throat.

"This is hard," he said at last. "We'll keep it short."

"I appreciate that, sir."

"Sergeant Winters and the officers on scene mentioned that you might have some insight into Sergeant Jones's shooting."

Guin was momentarily caught off guard.

She half-shrugged. "I told him everything. Or at least I think I did."

"He said you were pretty torn up." Briggs bounced his pen on the desk blotter. "So...did you or did you not see who fired the shots?"

Guin studied him, didn't want to take too long to answer. "No, sir. I did not."

He poised his pen, started jotting. "So, Sergeant Jones was dead when you discovered her."

"Yes sir. And the suspect had already fled."

Briggs's thick brow furrowed and he shook his head. "Then I don't understand. You provided Sergeant Winters with a description of the alleged shooter, but you're telling me you didn't see the suspect and Jones had already passed."

Oh boy. Guin was too rattled to think this quickly on her

feet. She cleared her throat, took a second stab at it. "Sergeant Jones told me as she passed."

Briggs's pen dropped to the blotter as if he could tell something forthcoming would never make it to the report. The Captain's look said he'd already heard an interesting version of this story from Winters. More than likely he'd blamed high-running emotions, figured he'd get the straight scoop out of her. And now here she was, talking in the same circles Winters had been. He looked like he'd really rather not hear it.

"Officer Marcus, if she had already…passed, as you previously stated, then how is it possible she spoke to you?"

Guin stared at him for a while. Everyone on scene had witnessed her total meltdown. Probably word was already all over the station that she thought she was seeing dead people. God knows what she'd babbled in the heat of the moment. She swallowed hard, told him, "It was her spirit."

Briggs didn't flinch. He didn't look thrilled to death, but to his credit, he only patiently waited for her to elaborate.

"She told me the suspect had on a black racing shirt, with a number twelve on it."

"Anything else?" he asked at last.

Guin hesitated. Nothing he needed to know. "No, nothing else, Captain."

"All right." Briggs replaced the form in his top drawer, withdrew a different one. Guin recognized it immediately and rolled her eyes.

"Marcus, it's been a bad day. I think some paid time off would be a really good thing, don't you?"

"And if I don't?" But she already could guess the answer. He ignored her lame inquiry, and continued filling out the paperwork. Guin still lobbied against it, but the argument lacked much zest. "Honestly, Captain, it's okay. I'll be fine. I just need a shower." She left out the part about needing a drink.

"No," he firmly answered. "I'm getting old, Marcus. I've had a lot of years seeing a lot of officers lose their partners and it's never easy." He signed the form, handed it to her. "Take this to personnel, I'll call Lisa and tell her to wait for you. Do it before you go to the crime lab."

Protocol said she had to leave her clothes with the lab after an officer-involved shooting. She was surprised they hadn't insisted upon it when they'd collected her boots. Guin glanced at the form. "A month? Captain…"

"This is a good thing, Marcus." He stood up, allowing his full height to cast an imposing shadow over her. "No arguments. Check in with me every week and keep me posted."

"And what the hell am I supposed to do for a month?"

"Yoga, vacation, knit yourself a damned sweater—I don't care what you do, as long as you're not doing it at my station."

Guin's shoulders softened. There was no fighting a direct order. She let her chin fall to her chest, expelled a sigh in the process. "One request, please?"

"What is it, Marcus?"

She raised her eyes back to his. "I would appreciate it that when you reassign me, that it would be with a male officer?"

"I'll take your request under consideration."

"Thank you, Captain." She started to shake his hand, realized she was a walking Hazmat concern, and dropped it back down at her side. "I'll see Lisa before I go to the lab."

It was really all he wanted to hear. Briggs nodded. He saw her to the door.

First stop, personnel. Then to the crime lab to leave her clothes. Then, wearing something a half-step up from disposable paper clothing, she'd find her way to a shit bar. There she planned to drink until she had nerve enough to go home to a bed sprinkled with rose petals; an unprecedented, ridiculously romantic gesture she'd made in advance for a date that would never, ever happen.

CHAPTER SEVEN

She stayed drunk for two days. It was her only way to cope. She'd have probably sobered up sooner, but she'd managed to finagle two bottles of Jose Cuervo off the sleazy bar owner the night she'd commenced her post-shooting binge. He'd told her it was against policy, then took pity on her, armed her with the tequila and settled her into a cab at two in the morning.

Two days later, she figured she should retrieve her car before it wound up at city impound and they came looking for her. She was in no mood for company, had already ducked several calls, including Terence. But he knew how she operated, respected that, and would give her a few days before pounding on her door.

Guin pulled the hood of her sweatshirt over her head and slunk into the backseat of the cab. She directed the driver to drop her at the gym. It sounded better than giving him the bar address at such an early hour of the day. When the driver pulled away, she jogged across the adjoining lots.

There was a chance that someone would eventually do a goodwill check to see why she'd not answered her phone. Knowing this, after she retrieved her car, Guin bypassed home and headed for the only other place she'd ever felt safe.

As usual, Granny June was in her garden. When she saw Guin, she abandoned her spade and embraced her granddaughter.

"Oh, sugar," she cooed in her ear. "I'm so, so sorry. I knew there was something."

Guin flipped the hood of her sweatshirt back, stiffened slightly and drew back to see her grandmother's eyes. "Why didn't you say something to me? I could have…have stopped it or something."

Granny June shook her head, led Guin by the hand to a bench swing and patted the seat next to her. "I had a vision you'd have a tough day, but it wasn't clear. Now I understand why."

Guin didn't understand anything anymore. "It makes no sense—I got nothing at all! Why didn't I see anything?"

Granny June turned wistful. "Well, honey, the closer you are to someone, the less you see. That's why I couldn't tell you what would be happening to you, because I didn't know myself."

"But why Cheryl, Granny? I don't get it."

The old woman patted her hand. "We're not supposed to get it. It was just her time."

"It was not her time!" Guin practically spat, tears burning behind her eyes again. "She was young and healthy! She had kids, for chrissakes."

"I know, I know, child." They sat quietly, the mood blanketed by Guin's sorrow.

"I saw her." She glanced at her grandmother.

"You saw her spirit?" Granny June's voice lacked surprise. She nodded, softly said, "That happens sometimes with the ones closest to you."

"Then why couldn't I see anything before that? Anything that would have warned me what was going to happen?" Tears spilled at last. Guin swiped them away with the backside of her hand. "What is the purpose of this…this power?"

Granny June sighed deeply, looked tired, old. "I know you two were close. That's the risk you run when you allow people in." She chuckled softly, turned misty. "If we knew what was to come every minute of every day, we'd never put a child on a school bus, never let them go anywhere or let them live their lives fully. That's not growth, that's not life. It's really a protection for us, you see? Otherwise life would only be pain, precaution... worry..."

Guin was not comforted by her words. "A little insight would be nice," she finally mumbled.

"So did you request some time off?"

Guin found her strength, her voice building as she thought about it. "Captain gave me a month-long time-out."

"That's plenty of time for a good rest." Granny June smiled sweetly. "Maybe it's just what the doctor ordered."

"Captain Briggs thinks I'm crazy."

Granny flipped her hand airily. "Well, poop on him. We know you're not crazy. Take care of yourself. You need to. Do something for yourself."

"Yeah, okay." Guin nodded, rolled her eyes. "I'll have all sorts of time to embrace this wonderful gift of mine."

Guin leaned over, rested her chin in the palm of her hand. Granny June scooted closer, stroked her back soothingly. Guin knew she was going to cry all over again. She wondered if her pain would abate any after Cheryl's funeral. It didn't feel like it could be that simple. She wondered if she was destined to grieve and be unhappy and alone.

"I gotta go." Guin made the quiet announcement. She blotted her face before her grandmother could see that she'd been crying again. They both stood, Guin edging toward the driveway. "I'll come back by in the next few days."

"Come by anytime, love, you know that."

"I will. I know." Guin forced a smile, gave a little wave, turned and lightly jogged down the driveway.

Guin closed the front door of her house behind her, killed

the porch light and the only interior lamp as well. She peeled the brown wrapper that had been hugging a fresh bottle of tequila and tossed it in the garbage. She went to the kitchen and returned with a glass and candle. In dim flickering candlelight, she downed a strong shot and set her glass on the end table. The liquor burned all the way down, warmed her thoroughly, but didn't quite do the trick. Getting drunk seemed ineffective as hell. She poured another, tossed it back, stared at the empty glass.

She extinguished the candle, abandoned the tiny living room, and peeled her clothes off, leaving a trail all the way to the bedroom. Setting the tequila on her nightstand, she collapsed onto the bed. In boxers and shirt, she lay staring at the ceiling, sipping straight from the bottle.

She had no idea how much time had passed, but Guin finally knew she was sufficiently insulated by a protective seal of tequila.

She blinked awake some time later, thankful that it was still night. She sighed, reached for the pillow next to her and plumped it. The action released a hint of the unmistakable scent of Cheryl's cologne. Immense sadness washed through her, chasing the miniscule joy the initial discovery had created. She clutched the pillow against her chest and began drifting in and out of sleep.

Cheryl stood beside the bed keeping an afterlife watch over her lover. When Guin's eyes opened, it occurred to her that she was simply drunk. Nonetheless, she edged over a bit and patted the space beside her. Cheryl smiled and got into bed.

Something jarred her from an alcohol-induced slumber. Guin blinked, wondered at first if she was hearing things. She drew back the covers and rubbed her eyes. It was pounding, and this time it wasn't coming from her head.

Guin sighed deeply, rose up and padded over her trail of clothes that led to the living room.

"What the fuck?" she muttered at the incessant hammering. She cleared her throat, weakly called out, "I'm coming."

She gave her house a cursory glance. It had looked better. She looked down at what she was wearing—still in her undies—

and then peeked out the curtained window. Beth was winding up for another round of pounding. Guin unlocked the door and the woman angrily burst in, charged past her, suitcase in tow.

"Hello?" Guin looked bewildered, slumped onto the couch.

Beth lowered her chin, dealt her a glare. "I've been waiting at the airport for more than an hour. I finally took a cab over here."

"Okay."

When the pieces didn't snap together quickly enough, Beth's impatience flared again. She waved her hand for effect. "It's Tuesday."

Guin ran the calendar through her muddled brain. Rubbed her forehead, and cringed.

"What have you been doing?" Beth walked an arc around her, examined the floor and the clothes. "Did you just get home?"

"No...I had a rough couple of days." She closed the door.

"Tell me about it." Beth dropped her garment bag onto the nearest chair, set her purse on top of that, shimmied out of her coat. "Express Air has monkeys for pilots. Talk about the worse turbulence ever—" As if seeing Guin for the first time, Beth stopped and peered at her, her face sobering at Guin's obvious and deep anguish. "Guin, what is it?"

"Cheryl was killed."

"Oh my God! What—what..." Beth was at a loss, suddenly realizing how selfish she must have appeared.

"We were on a call."

Beth's long strides bridged the gap in seconds. She pulled Guin to her, stroked her hair. "Oh baby. I'm so grateful you weren't hurt."

Guin nodded, couldn't think of anything fitting to say. Beth drew back slightly, looked into her eyes.

"Why didn't you call me?"

Guin blinked, shrugged slightly. "Should I have?"

Her words restored the cold room tone.

"Well, that's great," Beth said, stepping away from the embrace. "Nice to know I'm needed."

Guin stared at her hands, remembered them being blood spattered. She clenched her fists, released them as she breathed out, trying to refrain from pointing out Beth's dire need to be the center of the universe, even at a time like this. That in and of itself was a great tragedy.

She reined in her emotions, downgraded the much-deserved chastising to a simple, "This really isn't about you, Beth."

Beth appeared to mull it over, made peace with it, and nodded. "You're right." She approached Guin again, continued stroking her hair. "You're right about that."

Guin relaxed some as Beth wrapped her arms around her, soaking in the much-needed comfort. She stared at the floor, at a single blackened rose petal that had somehow survived her harried cleanup. She studied it as she recounted events in a dull narrative. "I just keep seeing it, rolling it around my head. It was awful. It happened so fast."

"You're not blaming yourself, are you?"

"No." It was probably the one thing she wasn't feeling. "No, she made me stay behind."

"That's when it happened?" Beth held her closer, whispered, "I don't know what I'd do if something happened to you. I missed you more than ever last weekend. It was really hard to get settled back in while I had you in my head."

And suddenly Guin remembered the other woman in Beth's life.

"Hard to get settled in with Jenn?"

Beth glanced to the side, clearly deciding whether to own it or not. She nodded once, as if it was a secret never kept; as if Guin should accept it, move on.

Guin felt a change come over her. She toed the rose petal and dragged it a few inches, shoved it beneath the ottoman where Beth would not see it. Guin was suddenly feeling restless and needy. She was feeling. It was a welcome change after endless hours of mind-numbing pain and drunken oblivion.

She grabbed Beth's wrists and pushed her hard up against the wall. She kissed her, hard, nibbled her lip, worked her way to her ear, demanded hungrily, "You missed me? Show me."

She pulled her toward the bedroom, where she attacked her wildly. She used Beth as a release for all her pain and hurt. Not one inch of her body was neglected on Guin's adrenalin-induced attack.

CHAPTER EIGHT

Guin stared at the red digital numbers on her bedside clock. By seven o'clock she and Beth had turned each other inside out several times. Guin felt spent, more emotionally than physically. She lay there listening to her lover whisper on the phone to her pregnant New York girlfriend, and that certainly wasn't helping the situation any. Beth had answered the call and had skittered off to the kitchen where she'd been ever since, talking in low, soothing tones.

"I know baby. Yeah, the flight was a little rough." Beth paused while the sound of a sunshiny sweet voice buzzed on the other end. Guin couldn't make it out, but it was happy sounding, and it even inspired Beth to chuckle softly. "Well, not to worry. This case is almost wrapped up and then I'll be back home."

Guin scooted to the edge of the bed, found her tank and

pulled it over her head. She felt around for her briefs, found Beth's slip, forced herself to clutch it and waited to see what it would tell her. She clearly saw Beth embrace a young, glowing woman, thrilled at being reunited with her bi-coastal lawyer girlfriend. She giggled, happily touched her belly. So much to tell her. She'd taken a cab to greet her at the airport...

Guin dropped the garment and the vision vanished. She laughed at herself. What in the hell was she doing fucking Beth?

Beth with a young girlfriend on the opposite coast who troubled to show up at the airport, on time, no doubt. By comparison, her West Coast girl wasn't quite up to snuff and was needy besides.

"I know, I know. And I don't want to miss a thing either." Beth's voice interrupted her thoughts. "Make yourself a nice cup of tea and get some rest, okay baby? I love you too. No, I love you more. No, I do..."

Guin rolled her eyes, thought she might convulse on the spot. She stood and stretched, fought off a looming headache and rummaged for something to wear. Moments later, a scantily clad Beth returned to the room to find Guin in jeans and a sweater. She froze in her tracks.

"What are you doing?" she asked at last.

"I have some things to do."

"At this hour?" Beth took a step closer. "I came clear across the country to spend time with you."

Guin started to collect Beth's things, felt a glimmer of a vision when she picked up the same slip, clenched her eyes shut and heaped the pile of clothing into Beth's arms.

"I have got to get out of your think-space," Guin muttered as she headed for the door.

Beth looked baffled, tipped her head slightly, disdain evident in her voice. "What did you just say?"

"Never mind." Guin raised her hands in surrender. "No more. I can't do this."

"Do what?"

"You." Guin went to the closet, hunted around the floor for her boots, remembered the crime lab had them. She grabbed a pair of tennis shoes instead. "I can't be the other woman. It's not my style."

Beth dropped the clothes on the bed, put her hands on her perfect hips. "I thought you liked it because there were no strings."

"Yeah." Guin shoved her feet in the shoes, didn't bother to tie them. "But not when your girlfriend in New York is pregnant and about to start a family with you."

Beth was too stunned to deny it. "How did you know that?"

"Doesn't matter." Guin hastily raked her fingers through unruly curls. She grabbed her wallet and shoved it in her jeans pocket. She adjusted the hem on her sweater. "Just go back to her. Hopefully she won't find out about any of this."

She left Beth standing in her house, got into her car and drove.

Though she didn't much care where she went, she found that when she was in a mood like this, she always ended up at the same place.

Sometime after midnight she called Terence from the bar.

"I need you to come get me."

"Where in the hell have you been?" He'd clearly been asleep but was quickly coming to life. "What—you just fall off the radar and don't tell your friends?"

"I know, I know." She cut off his concerned lecture. She apologized for waking him, and then gave him directions to the bar.

"I'll be there within the hour."

"Thanks," she said. "Oh, and bring a suit. I can't go alone tomorrow."

He knew exactly what she meant.

The sound of "Taps" being played alerted Guin that the funeral was drawing to an end. As such things tend to be, it was depressing as hell, made more so by Cheryl's husband and children looking shell-shocked and numb with grief. She'd zoned out three minutes after start time to protect herself from feeling too much. The cemetery was lined with officers in solemn formation gathered to pay their last respects. Three shots fired in succession by an honor guard symbolized that the casket would be lowered into the ground. Gone.

Gone, the most loving relationship in her life. She wondered if Frank had any idea how much they had in common. She glanced at Terence when everyone began to file past the widower to shake hands, embrace or offer kind words of sympathy.

"You've got to do it," he said.

For a layman, he was doing a good job of reading her mind. She sighed and started toward the processional. Terence gave a friendly nod to a few officers across the way, but Guin pretended to not notice anyone. Terence spoke quietly to her as the line moved along, closer to the grieving family. "It was a nice service. Good turnout."

She nodded. It was necessary small talk designed to soothe her frayed emotions. They arrived at Frank who surprised her by pulling her into his sturdy embrace. He wept on her shoulder for a moment before she robotically put her arms around him, patted his back as best she should. Her conscience kicked into overtime when she looked at the young boys, four years apart in age. The two of them stood like exaggerated stairsteps, quietly bewildered after the heart-wrenching events of the day.

Guin had to say something. Terence nodded encouragement.

"I'm...sorry for your loss, Frank." She repeated the same words Briggs had said to her days earlier. He let go of her at last, leaned back, nodded. Guin struggled to follow up his unexpected emotional display, felt guilty as hell. "How are things?"

"As good as can be expected." Frank gave the boys a look, forced a smile. "Right guys? We're hanging tough."

Seeing her evident struggle, Terence swooped in, clasped Frank's hand and introduced himself. They made small talk as Guin knelt before the boys. It might very well be the last time she'd see them. "Hey guys. Rough day, huh?"

The littlest one stepped into her arms easily, and Guin was surprised for the second time in a handful of minutes. She hoped neither of them would mention that she'd not been at their house for a while. She and Cheryl had done well in keeping their relationship low-profile around the children. As far as they knew, Guin was a good friend of Mommy's, nothing more.

"Who's this?" Guin said, tugging the ear of a teddy bear in Michael's clutches.

"Mr. Bear."

Guin feigned approval, shook the bear's fuzzy, well-worn hand. "A pleasure to meet you, Mr. Bear."

"He likes hugs too." With that, young Michael thrust the bear at her. She couldn't believe how amazingly brave the boys were, even at a time like this. Cheryl had done an excellent job with them. Michael commanded her, "Hug him."

Guin held the bear close and was suddenly overwhelmed by the story it told her. She was right there, watching Cheryl as she tucked her sons into bed for the night. She pressed the bear under Michael's arm, kissed his forehead. Stroked the boy's long bangs out of his dark eyes.

"Good night, big guy."

"I don't want to start school, Mommy," he whined. Cheryl sat on the edge of his bed, smiling.

"Sure you do. You're going to love it. Wait and see."

Michael paused, looked more than concerned, trusted her implicitly. "If you say so."

"I do say so."

Guin handed the bear back to Michael as fast as she could, eager to break contact with it. Michael looked at her strangely as she touched her lips, choked back tears.

"You okay?"

Leave it to Cheryl's son to ask after her well-being in the darkest hours of his young life. Guin nodded, quickly flicked her tears away with the back of her hand. She smiled, stroked Michael's bangs out of his eyes just like she'd seen his mother do; spoke to him the same way, too.

"I am okay. And you will be too. You wait and see."

Michael regarded her with the same weary eyes. "If you say so."

"I do say so." She pulled the child into a quick hug, whispered, "So long, big guy."

She released the boy and left them quickly. Terence had to run a little to catch up. She had wiped her tears and a little dollop of makeup onto her uniform sleeve. Terence knew it was the bear. He didn't offer comfort, only put an arm around her and led her silently to his car.

A whirlwind of problems were occurring in her life and resolving themselves at a rapid-fire pace. There was Beth and Beth's girlfriend, the baby-mama, and Guin's subsequent departure from that relationship. Then, of course, there was Cheryl's departure.

It was a crushing blow dealt to someone who felt she deserved it. She was practically a home-wrecker. But it was more than that and she couldn't walk away from it so easily. Cheryl had left behind her entire young family.

Guin had bypassed all offers of attending the wake or dinner with her colleagues. She went home, slept off her drunk before she'd started it. And when she did start, it lasted for four days.

Terence, sick of her ignoring his calls, pounded on her door until his knuckles were raw. At last he headed to the main house where he was able to flash his badge and obtain a key.

When he let himself in, she was sitting on the couch. Unfazed by his entrance, she waved for him to sit down across from her. Looking more than a little pissed, he dropped into the opposite chair.

"I thought I was going to find you with the business end of a pistol in your face."

She shrugged, had honestly considered that it would be preferable to this pain-filled alternative. "They took my gun from me."

Terence nodded. "Briggs was wise to do that." He looked around, surveying the place. "You have any other weapons beside your service?"

She shook her head.

"You eat?" He eyed her gaunt frame, amended his inquiry. "At all anymore?"

She shrugged again.

"That's it, this is ridiculous." He clapped his hands together, took his jacket off, tossed it aside. "Snap out of it. I'm ordering some pasta or Thai food or something."

She only sat there.

"What the hell, Guin? Pity much?" He was exasperated. "This is shit—we both know it. You're going to sit around here and boohoo for the entire month?" He picked up two empty liquor bottles, carted them to the kitchen and dropped them with a clang into an empty garbage can. He opened her empty refrigerator, checked her bare cupboards, found a half-empty package of crackers. "Just as I thought. Liquid diet. You're turning into a full-fledged drunk. Not attractive."

"I'm not drunk," she finally defended herself, as she did whenever the subject of her drinking arose. "I was just...enjoying a cocktail by the pool."

He appeared in the doorway, popped the top button on his shirt. "Yeah, well, last time I checked the pool was on the other side of those doors. Maybe it's a good thing you haven't eaten. I'm not sure you'd get off your ass to use the bathroom."

This remark amused Guin. She pictured herself boozing it up, wallowing in her own feces, surrounded by cats that would one day eat her. Tidy. She tipped her head thoughtfully at the notion. "I should get some cats."

Terence grabbed his cell phone out of his jacket pocket, hit a speed dial and ordered noodles with vegetable tofu, low on the spice. He disappeared into the kitchen and returned with a water bottle. He handed it to her.

"Drink up. You're dehydrated. Your skin looks a hundred years old."

"You always know how to cheer me up, Terence."

He dropped back into the chair. "Yeah, well, you always know how to scare the hell out of me. Answer your phone. Hell—answer your mother-fucking door."

They were silent for several minutes.

Terence rolled up his shirt sleeves, leaned forward onto his knees, speaking confidentially. "You have any more visions?"

She shook her head. "This is my safe place. I've eliminated everything Cheryl from here—everything, everyone." She unscrewed the cap, took a long chug of the water. "Nobody can get to me here."

"And that's why you're existing on tequila and saltines." He nodded. "You could have called me, you know. Just at least to let me know you were doing the whole pity hibernation thing."

"I actually couldn't have. My phone's toast."

"How?"

"It got damp."

"Modern technology is hard to kill. The battery probably just needs drying out." Terence started to rise. "Where's it at?"

"Bottom of the pool."

He sat back down. "Tell me you did not get a vision from your phone."

"No, but I got a lot of calls I didn't want to answer." She studied him, let him believe his was one of them for only a moment before she explained herself. "It's Beth. I'm not...with her anymore."

He brightened significantly. "Well, that's the first good news I've heard all week."

"I have nobody now, and you call that good news?"

"No, that's the bad news." He stood, and slid right next to her in the oversized chair, held her close despite her unwillingness to be held. "You know what the good news is?"

"You're going to go back to your own chair?" she said, eyes wide with discomfort.

"You've got great hair." He lowered his chin, reassessed her curly mop. "Normally. And you've got a cute little button nose. A firm ass, gorgeous gams..."

Guin's smirk turned into a reluctant smile. "You're a dope."

"But I'm here."

And suddenly he'd turned serious. Guin's smile faded as she considered it. Perhaps it was time to get out of the house, breathe in and out, exercise her...gams. She hated pathetic people, didn't want to be one. Lonely and sex-starved, perhaps. But she didn't want to be pathetic. Truth be known, she wouldn't be sex-starved for long. She settled back against her friend, sighed.

Terence muttered, "And you're the dope."

"Thanks, Terence."

CHAPTER NINE

"Do you keep a little flower garden at your own place, Guin?"

Granny June came out to the bistro set with two glasses of iced tea. She handed one to Guin then took a seat across from her.

"My own place is not even my own. So no." She took a sip; she felt physically spent after a third day in a row of trimming and transplanting Granny's garden. Their labors had paid off in a paradise of blossoms.

"Everyone needs a little haven, I always say."

"That's why I come here," Guin remarked, smiling at her grandmother. In reality her safe haven had less to do with the atmosphere and more to do with Granny June.

"So, how have you been keeping yourself busy with all this

time off you have?" Granny slipped her gloves off, shook the dirt from them and laid them on the tiny table. She didn't ask of vacations or other things one might normally be inclined to do during a leave of absence. She knew what was on Guin's mind. "Have you had any more visions of your friend?"

Guin's eyes involuntarily widened. "Could you see that?"

"No, child." The old woman took a sip of tea, shrugged. "But why else would you be elbows deep in mulch for this many days straight? Your old granny recognizes self-administered therapy when she sees it. Not that I don't appreciate the company. Or the help."

Guin looked thoughtful. "I'm not having any visions. They were kind of a source of comfort for me for a while, but I ran out of things to...touch."

Granny reached across the table, clasped her granddaughter's hand. "My love. It will get better."

"It can't get worse, that's for sure."

"Now, you and I know that's not true. That's why we've got to enjoy every minute of it, every day." She rose, retrieved her clippers from inside a nearby flowerpot. Granny talked as she walked to the nearest flowery row. "That's why you've got this time to yourself. You take the time to mourn and appreciate what you've lost. Then hopefully you take something good away from it and you remember it for next time you try to fall in love."

"Am I that obvious, Granny?" Guin's face felt warm. Granny knew Cheryl was married. None of this was helping her conscience any. "I didn't mean to fall in love with her."

"I know, child. We never do," she called from the other side of the row. In moments she approached Guin, handed her a small bouquet. "Here you go. Your own personal garden."

Guin smiled, took the flowers and stood to give her grandmother a hug.

"How can you be so different from Mom?" Guin whispered in her ear.

If she'd caught Granny June off guard with her question, it didn't show. She squeezed Guin's hand in her own tinier one. "Gloria has always been...a different case. I used to blame myself for it all the time—my blessing was her curse." Granny smiled in the sunlight. "All those years I spent at Heart House trying to help all those children, and I couldn't even help my own daughter. It felt so hypocritical of me."

Granny rarely spoke of her former career rescuing homeless families off the streets and steering them toward a more meaningful life. Guin figured her humility about those acts made her as close to an angel on earth as one could get.

"But one day she brought me this beautiful, sensitive granddaughter who I've watched grow into a fine woman." Granny winked at Guin, whispered, "And that alone is worth anything Gloria could dish out to this old woman."

"I love you, Granny." Guin smiled at Granny, buried her nose in the sweet-smelling blooms.

"Now go home and get these in some water." Granny eyed her dirt-covered granddaughter. "And soak yourself when you're done doing that. You're not used to my kind of workout."

Guin feigned offense. "Are you saying you're tougher than me?"

"We both have our dirty work." Granny smiled, added, "I'd take mine any day over yours, though."

"So, I'll see you tomorrow?"

"No. Tomorrow's the day you do something for you." Granny's voice conveyed that she meant business. "Me and this garden—we're just your tether. Now cut the line and see what's going on in the rest of this world. And that's an order."

At home, there was a note taped to her door.

Going to Masquerades. Meet me there? xo-T

Guin snatched the note and went inside. The last thing she felt like doing was going to a noisy bar to meet her goofy friend with his short attention span. She looked around the kitchen for anything that would serve as a vase, and she found an old glass jelly jar with Tweety Bird on it. She filled it with water and plunked the flowers into it, fanned them out nicely.

She showered until her skin was adequately pruned. She towel-dried her hair as she entered the kitchen. She inspected every cupboard, every shelf of the refrigerator. Empty. Her eyes roved the countertop and landed on Terence's scribbled note. She sighed and went to get dressed.

An hour later she was seated in a too-noisy bar, sipping tequila. Terence was nowhere in sight.

"Figures," she muttered.

"Pardon?" The voice came from over her shoulder, and as noisy as it was, Guin wasn't even sure it was directed at her. Then a woman with flaming scarlet hair and matching dress leaned over her small table. "I hope you were saying your date didn't show."

Guin looked at her, half-smiled, shook her head. "My friend didn't show."

"Her loss," the woman purred.

"His loss, actually."

The woman looked utterly surprised at her bad call. Guin chuckled, figured the mistake was convenient and didn't bother to correct it. She wasn't in the mood for company anyway.

"Too bad," she said, and she was back on the prowl, disappearing into the crowd like a ghost.

Guin expelled the breath she'd been holding. "Holy shit..." she muttered much more quietly this time. She flagged down the waitress, motioned for one more. Her eyes then slid past the waitress down to a patron seated on a barstool across the room. An African-American woman she thought she recognized made eye contact with her for several seconds. Guin craned her neck, tried to get a better look, a feat made difficult thanks to a flamboyant fellow waving a feather boa on the cramped dance floor. When the boa finally moved, the woman was gone. The waitress returned and slid the drink in front of Guin, startling her. She passed her a ten, tossed back the shot, and looked around the room for the woman. She was as gone with the wind as Scarlet.

Guin swiped the back of her hand across her damp lips, pulled her jacket on and slipped out of her seat. She silently cursed her absent friend all the way to the exit of the firetrap bar. She was hungry and considered that if she'd not loused up the chance, she could be having the woman with cherry hair helping soothe her various appetites. But it was probably for the best.

On the way home she stopped at a grocery store, bought brown rice, California rolls, pumpkin granola and tequila. She went home and plopped in front of the television for what had become another exciting night in the life of Guin Marcus.

After a week of solitude, she called Terence.

"You got a new phone?" he squealed.

"I tried my tin can with string, but you wouldn't pick up."

"Funny girl," he said, then, "Where were you the other night?"

"I was there."

Terence laughed. "You're kidding me. I never dreamed you'd show. I ran into an old friend outside. We never even made it through the door."

"Thanks. You could have left me a message."

"On what phone? Your tin can with string?" he scoffed. "Did you have fun? Get lucky?"

"No, and no." She leaned back onto the couch, considered what she was dying to ask her friend. She'd resisted until now. Mustering up as impartial tone as possible, she went for it. "So, did they find the guy?"

He didn't need to ask which guy.

"Guin, you know I can't talk to you about that."

"Why the fuck not?" All notions of cool went out the door. She sat up, raked her hand through curly hair. "I was her partner. I was on the call. I was a witness. That's not protocol. You're out of line."

"Just calm down." Terence sounded like he was thinking it over. Guin listened to his breathing through the phone, suddenly saw him outside a Starbucks in West Hollywood. Weird.

"Are you...getting coffee?"

"Why? Do I sound overly-caffeinated?" was his monotone response.

"No more than usual." She'd think about it later. More pressing matters were presently at hand. "So, what about the case?"

"Of course it's not protocol to deny you information." His voice grew quiet and she could see that he was surrounded by a few other java seekers. "I'm just looking out for your well-being. I'd love to think that you could really capitalize on this time off. Really get this junk out of your head."

Guin heard him mouth thank you to the lady behind the counter. Maybe she saw him do it—who could say? It was getting weirder by the moment. The idea of him telling her to clear the junk out of her head was funny—hell, she couldn't even get him out of her head.

"So, talk to me," she persisted.

"I'll check the progress."

"That's all I'm asking."

"You could call Briggs yourself, you know." He took a sip. "He said for you to check in with him."

"I'm not calling him. I'm pissed at him."

"What for?"

"He suspended me, duh."

"Not a suspension—paid leave."

"Same difference."

She was growing impatient, wondered if she needed to get to a store for more supplies since she could feel another lockdown coming on.

"How about I come over." He sounded like his heart wasn't in it. Plus, Guin knew that if he'd trekked all the way over to WeHo, he was meeting someone. Besides, she felt like bad company. No sense in poisoning her friend.

"No, do your thing. I'm going to bed early."

They said their goodbyes and Guin stared at her phone. The faint vision of him drinking coffee vanished with the disconnect. She considered the real possibility that her gift was evolving. She ran her finger along the phone, looked thoughtful, and finally punched in Cheryl's cell number. Promptly an automated operator said that the line was no longer in service and she felt nothing at all. Guin pressed the off button, tossed her phone down, watched it bounce off the couch and land on the rug.

She looked at her watch. Nearly four o'clock and she was restless. She'd prided herself on the fact that she'd never been enough like her mother to pop even a sleeping pill. However, an innocent Benadryl might do the trick... Of course the interim between taking the cold meds and waiting for it to kick into snooze-time would require lying in a bed that had managed to capture Beth. Bully for her. No amount of sheet-washing would exorcise those demons. She wondered if there was a market for Tide with Spirit Cleanser.

If only she could control the visions. If she must be haunted, she could ask for a haunting of a different nature. A Cheryl nature.

CHAPTER TEN

On her first day back at work, Guin tapped on Captain Briggs's office door and waited for him to wave her in. She removed her hat and took the seat before his desk.

"Captain."

His clasped hands rested on his blotter and regarded her appraisingly. "So, Marcus, how was your time off?"

"Fine, thanks." But she could control her expressions about as well as she could control her visions.

"I'm very glad to get you back on patrol."

"Me too, sir." She forced her tone softer. "I'm ready."

"Good to hear." Captain Briggs studied her for a moment, and she could tell he was making a decision. It puzzled her. At last he reached into his desk drawer and set a small box in front of her. His voice lost some of its rigid authority. "Before we move on, I thought you might like to have these."

Guin blinked, furrowed her brow. She removed the lid to find Cheryl's badge and name pin. She stared at it for several seconds. "I don't understand—how...?"

"Frank came in and took what he wanted. It was as if he purposely left them behind. I took the liberty to acquire them."

"Thank you, Captain." She was dying to touch them, but wanted to save it for later when she could be alone. She hurriedly closed the box, stuck it in her pocket. Her next words sounded squeaky. "I appreciate it. Truly."

His smile was fleeting, rare. "And we caught the guy."

Guin's eyes eagerly met his as she anticipated his explanation.

"Look, I don't know what this means, but from the looks of the garbage in his garage, he likes racing."

The number twelve racing shirt.

Guin's heart quickened. He nodded in acknowledgment that her unusual encounter turned out to be correct, then quickly turned all-business, a silent message that they wouldn't speak of such improbable things again. Guin looked away, sending her response that it was already off her mind. As if.

Briggs cleared his throat, indicating the end of their personal "chat" and the commencement of official business. "So, you've got a new partner."

She sat up a little straighter. She was far better with business over personal. "Yeah, I heard it might be Burnette."

"No, actually Clive just made detective. He's out of the running."

"Oh." Guin's eyes reflected her disappointment at him. The air in the room turned...odd.

"We've had some incoming transfers from other units."

"Wait—what about Burnette's old partner, Sergeant Winters?"

"Winters has already been reassigned." Briggs started shuffling paperwork on his desk, anything to avoid looking at her. She wondered why. "Officer Reese will be your new partner. The best choice among the available personnel."

Guin had never heard of him.

Captain Briggs jammed his thumb on the phone intercom. "Sara, could you please send in Officer Reese."

Guin comforted herself with the notion that come what may, it would be nice to get back on the street.

A knock on the door interrupted her thoughts, and she turned in her seat, a ready-made amiable smile plastered on her face.

Officer Reese was early thirties, olive skin, dark hair, boobs.

Guin's smile immediately melted off her face. She turned around in her seat so quickly she almost fell out of it. Despite whiplash, she issued her boss a death look. That went ignored.

"Officer Reese, you will be working with Officer Marcus. She's one of our best."

A thickly accented voice emerged from her perfect lips. "You can call me April."

April?

Reese took a step closer to Guin's chair. Briggs seemed impervious to the fact that Guin was scorching him with a fiery stare. Reese's hand had been extended for an introductory handshake for several long seconds. Finally, Guin turned in her seat, didn't bother to get up. Gave her a limp handshake. She couldn't help but notice April's slim fingers, smooth hands, toned arms in her short-sleeved uniform shirt, perfectly glossy long hair…

She was overwhelmed by a vision of the two of them in bed, kissing, touching… It buzzed through her head with such resounding force, Guin practically yanked her hand away. To say it was shocking was a serious understatement—after all, she'd just met the woman.

Oh, hell no.

Free of April's touch, she was angry at herself. And her boss.

April arched an eyebrow, glanced at the captain as if seeking verification that indeed this was the woman he'd paired her with. He easily read this, nodded at her, ignored every other awkward feeling abundant in the room.

"I'm sure you two will do well once you've gotten to know each other." Though he didn't sound sure of it at all.

"I'm sure we will." April said, confidence in her voice. Guin tried to place the woman's accent. New Zealand? Australia?

"Let me know how it goes." And just like that, Briggs washed his hands of the situation. Guin still stared at him, waited for him to make even the remotest eye contact with her so she could at least get in a nasty look. He knew this, didn't cave. "That will be all, officers. Have a good first day out."

The end.

Just as Briggs had done to her, Guin refused to look into April's eyes. She dared not even accidentally touch her again. She even breathed through her mouth to avoid getting another whiff of the woman's clean, fresh scent.

Fuck me running, she thought.

By noon, the morning had lasted forever.

Guin fumbled with her keys at the door of her tiny house. She normally wasn't quite so uncoordinated, and kept nervously eyeing April who was following her, carrying their Mexican take-out. There would be no sexual shenanigans in this house today, no matter what any vision said. She hoped April understood this was strictly a pit stop.

"I can't believe I forgot my wallet," she muttered as a reminder. She shoved the right key in the lock, gave it a twist. "This'll just take a second."

"No big deal, Guin. We could have just eaten there." She shrugged, followed her new partner into the living room. Her tone was casual, friendly. "It's not like I don't know where to find you for payback."

"No, I'll get it now." She looked around, then back at her partner loaded down with their lunches. She hurriedly motioned toward the furniture. "Take a seat or something. Be right back."

Guin returned to find April already making herself comfortable, spreading their lunch out like an indoor picnic. It made her uneasy. She fanned out eight ones and handed it over. "That should do it. Thanks."

"No problem, as I said." April motioned for her to join her. "Let's eat. If we wait any longer it'll get cold."

They ate in silence, April casting little discomfited glances around her at Guin's sparse furnishings. Guin felt compelled to speak up. "What's wrong?"

"Nothing's wrong." April shook her head, added, "You lived here long?"

"Yeah, why?"

"I thought maybe you just moved in or something." She took another bite, looked around, waved her fork slightly. "There's nothing on your walls."

Guin was taken back to the day Cheryl had made a similar query.

"Are you a minimalist or something?"

Guin stared blankly at April, didn't know if her new partner had said it in her living room or her old one had said it in her head. Given the difference in accent, she considered that it should have been a no-brainer. Everything was crashing into everything else. Jesus, she could be really losing her mind.

Guin snapped out of it, cleared her throat. "No. I've been here for three years and I like it this way."

"Gotcha."

They ate in silence until finally April set her carton down, and addressed Guin: "Look, I know I'm not Cheryl, but I am your new partner."

Guin stared at her, surprised that a new officer would refer to a superior officer in such a casual manner, albeit a deceased one. It was a blatant show of disrespect in her opinion.

"I know there's a lot going on with you," April said a little nervously, "I'm not sure it all has to do with your, uh, partner." April sidestepped the word "dead." She swallowed hard, as if focused on a mission. "It's just that I'm pretty good at reading people. It's kind of a special gift of mine."

Guin arched an eyebrow almost involuntarily. She considered the breadth of her own "special gift" and did her best not to laugh out loud. Cynicism was unattractive. Not that she was trying to be attractive. Not at all.

"I'd like to talk, but only if you want to or need to," April went on.

"Well, maybe with a whole lot of time and a whole lot of tequila."

"Sometime soon, I hope." She smiled, patted Guin's thigh lightly, a gesture surely nothing more than casual. Nonetheless, the vision was lightning-bolt powerful—she and April, in her bed, having sex. So alarmingly vibrant with much more detail than the last vision; much more passion than the previous one, too. The positions they were conspiring to create bordered on preposterous and had Guin's cheeks red with warmth. She felt her heart quicken. Jesus—she really had to get a grip.

April took her hand away, broke contact; her voice interrupted Guin's erotic reverie.

"Besides, I'm here to stay whether you like it or not." She sounded more confident having made her intentions known. She took a quick sip of her drink. Quietly she added, "Though I'd prefer you liked it. I'm not so bad."

Guin set her lunch aside, heard herself stammering, "Look, I never said that..." Obviously this woman was going to mean something to her if there was a roll in the hay involved. Not to mention that her vision had shown them performing daring acts one would not entrust to merely a casual romp. But Guin wanted privacy, craved solitude, and surely wasn't ready for anything more than that right now.

She considered that her own talents had been changing as of late. So in reality, who knew what all she was capable of? Perhaps she could defy the vision. After all, a relationship really wasn't in her best interest or April's. There was a slim chance her talents had expanded to picking up some lustful psychic vibe from April's mind. If that be the case, she needed to relay that message ASAP—this was to be a business-only partnership. Period.

She opened her mouth, forced anything commanding to come out. Instead, she heard, "You should try the salsa. It's really good."

So much for taking command.

"I'll try it." She reached across, scooped a chip into the salsa and gave it a whirl. Her eyes widened in genuine pleasure. "Wow, sí, sí…bueno."

The accent-scarred Spanish caused the corner of Guin's mouth to twitch into a funny half-smile.

"What?" April grinned.

"That's…the worst accent I've ever heard."

"Ah, cut me some slack. I only fell off the vegemite wagon a handful of years ago."

Guin tipped her head, curious. "Really? An Aussie?"

"Yeah. I came over to visit my aunt and never went back. Went to school and the rest is history."

Guin dabbed her lips with a paper napkin, grateful for the subject change. "And then you joined the LAPD?"

"Sure did. I watched a lot of X-Files. Maybe that's why I always dreamed of working for your FBI. But obviously being a non-native, that's not possible."

"Yeah. I forgot about that rule." Guin nodded, looked pensive, tipped her head to the side. "Well, it's not exactly the X-Files, but you'll find your share of aliens and freaks working the beat I work. Though they tend to be mostly illegals and transients from Venice Beach, but…"

April laughed hard, and Guin couldn't help but chuckle at the glorious sound.

"This works for me. I've always wanted to…" April's eyes playfully darted, her eyebrows wriggled, and she dropped her voice into a cartoon-like whisper, "…solve crimes."

"But, you're not a detective, so—"

"Not yet, but I will be someday. As soon as I put my time in here." She grabbed her uniform shirt with her thumb and index finger, thrusting her name badge and officer number forward for demonstrative purposes. She then let it go, shrugged lightly. "So now you know everything about me."

"I doubt I know everything," Guin heard herself say. In the wild event that April did have "a gift" she started moving around to avoid looking into the woman's eyes. She quickly balled up napkins, gathered their sacks and cartons and made her speedy exit to dump it all in the kitchen trash.

She leaned against the countertop, took a few deep breaths. She didn't want a female partner and now she had one. She didn't want to like April, and now she did. It had been a day of surprises.

The vision continued niggling in the back of her brain, and she desperately tried to force it out. It might mean nothing at all. She'd experienced that kind of thing before, like the time when… Okay, so she'd never experienced such a thing before.

Still, Granny June said the visions had purpose. It stood to reason that if someone was "blessed" with such a purpose, it would be to benefit the future, or at very least, it was a lesson to not repeat mistakes of the past. Right?

For some reason, she suddenly recalled her high school days and her mother's drunken wisdom whenever Guin would ask to go somewhere.

"No," she'd slur. "That's how nice girls end up dead."

It didn't make a lot of sense to her, but nothing her mother said ever did.

Guin took another deep breath. She needed some courage stronger than her own. She eyed the tequila bottle on the side counter, picked it up, looked at it wistfully. She sighed and put it in the cupboard with a silent promise to revisit it later.

Guin was determined to make this work, to not cave to whatever lustful intentions she or her partner could possibly be harboring, now or in the future. She would not end up in bed with April, if it took every last fiber of her being.

"No," she quietly reinforced her resolve aloud. "That's how nice girls end up dead."

CHAPTER ELEVEN

There were five channels on the television. That's all she could pilfer off the satellite dish for the main house. And truthfully it was only enough to get basic news (mostly bad) and check the weather (seasonally temperate). Guin, wearing a modified version of her earlier outfit, uniform pants with a tank top in place of shirt, tossed the remote aside and finished her beer. She pulled herself off the couch and wandered into the kitchen.

She set the bottle in the sink and got a fresh one, then leaned against the countertop to stare at the box for a while. The box. At last she removed the lid and stared at Cheryl's badge and pin.

It took the rest of the bottle and several minutes before she had the courage to take the nameplate out and hold it in her hand. When nothing happened right away, tears sprang to her eyes. She shut her eyes and held onto the pin tightly. She even willed herself to cry, to get it out, praying she would find some relief with an emotional release. Nothing. Until she opened her eyes, and jumped back at the sight before her.

Cheryl had materialized, stood there plain as day, wearing a uniform void of any damage. She smiled at her. Overwhelmed, Guin took a step closer to her.

"Cheryl?" she said in a small voice, then more strongly, "Cheryl. My God—it's you."

"Hi, Guin."

Guin wrapped her mind around the sweet sound of her lover's voice, felt warmth beyond anything human. Relief flooded through her. She shook her head, confused.

"But you're…"

"Dead," Cheryl confirmed.

For a moment, Guin hoped otherwise. She reached out to the ethereal presence, felt warmth instead of skin. She drew her hand back, looked her ghostly partner up and down.

"Your shirt—there's…no bullet holes."

"Sweetheart, you're only going to see what you want to see," Cheryl softly answered.

"I want to see you. Oh God—I so want to see you."

Cheryl's smile was effervescent. "I know. I'm here for you."

"What you said to me," Guin stammered. She nervously rubbed the name tag still in her clutches. "I wanted to tell you, I honestly did."

"I know, sweetheart."

"I just…"

"Guin," Cheryl said lovingly. "I already know."

Guin reached for Cheryl's hand. The energy contained there was breathtakingly powerful. Guin tried to absorb it. Her chest tightened, her breath caught in her throat, the effect almost painful as the energy wrapped around her. Jolted, she dropped the name tag and everything vanished at once.

Stunned, Guin looked around. "Cheryl?" She dropped to the floor and scooped the name tag into both hands, rubbed it. "Cheryl? Cheryl! No!"

She curled into a ball in the center of the floor, crying. "No,

Cheryl. Come back. Please, please baby take me with you. Please, please take me with you..."

Several hours and a shot of tequila later, a semi-recovered Guin sat across from Terence at his favorite bar, Masquerades. It was also quite possibly the loudest bar on the planet. Guin waved to the waitress for another. A shirtless bartender, obviously bent on catching Terence's attention, personally delivered the shots. Guin promptly downed hers, requested another. Things were beginning to blur. She looked at Terence, who was saying something to her.

"I can't hear you," she said, hand signaling around her ear. "Too fucking loud."

He leaned across the table, got right in her face, smiled. "I said, it was just a rumor."

"What rumor?" she hollered.

"There really isn't a tequila shortage." He tossed back his own shot, held up a second finger for the half-naked Boy Wonder to bring them refills. The fellow complied, eagerly trotting his Chippendale-worthy body back to their table. Terence paid, then tipped him more than the bill.

"These pretty boys are going to put you in the poorhouse," she told him. The two clinked shot glasses in the center of the table. Down the hatch. Two empty glasses hit the table with the same velocity. Terence slightly cringed and Guin laughed at him. "You're going to have to train if you want to drink with me, pretty boy-toy."

"No shit," he muttered over a lull in the music. Then he shot her a look when she waved two more fingers in the air. "Guin. Slow down."

"What?" She smiled, shrugged. The drinks were rapidly warming her, soothing her frayed nerves after her earlier encounter with Cheryl. She'd surely feel better once she could chalk it up to a drunken memory. Boy Wonder sailed across the bar again. Guin's tip was more modest than Terence's. She regarded her friend's expression, tried to pin it down to concern or disgust. "What? I gave him two bucks. I don't want in his pants."

The lingering Boy Wonder grinned big, seemingly satisfied

with the smaller tip. Terence gave him a signal with a finger across his throat that Guin should be cut off. Wonder winked, nodded, and a bunch of flirtation followed. Guin saw it all, rolled her eyes at their ridiculousness.

"I'm fine, Dad," she told him when they were alone again. She looked around at the number of obviously raring single ladies around them, smiled. "Someone else will gladly hook me up."

"Jesus, Guin. You scare me." He sipped the shot before him. She slammed hers. He cringed even more this time. "Yikes. So I take it your first week back was a little rougher than you'd have preferred?"

She thought it over for a millisecond. "Aside from my new partner—a booby-hot female, and the fact that everything I touch haunts the shit out of me, it's really been splendid. I'm ordering another."

She stuck her hand in the air, waved it until an attractive waitress came their way. Guin shot Terence a smug look, having overridden his order, and promptly asked for two tequilas.

"I'm not ready," Terence said.

"It's not for you." She handed the woman some cash when she returned and placed two fresh shots in front of her. "Thanks."

"You getting back on track then?" he asked her, ignoring her earlier assessment of her situation.

"Yep. Or at least I will be thanks to my friend here." She tipped one back.

"Seriously, do you think that's such a good idea?"

Guin grinned. "Well, Terence, you know what they say. A few drinks a day keeps the visions away."

"You are just a few shots away from me visiting you on your weekly pass."

"Rehab? Never."

"I was thinking a nice little place called Shady-something-or-other where they care for people who have lost their minds."

"Ah, the funny farm." She shrugged, picked up the second shot. "It'll be good to see mom again."

She actually had no idea where her mother was at the moment, but she could always be sure that when things were going good, good old dysfunctional mom was sure to make an appearance out of the blue. She was a ghost as much as Cheryl was and as crazy as Guin felt she herself was. Of course, crazy people never think they're crazy, Guin assured herself. That she often contemplated her own precarious sanity said that she probably wasn't as far gone as her mother was. Guin suspected that good old Mama-Gloria didn't possess the maturity of a seventeen-year-old. Then again, even a seventeen-year-old would know better than to lock a toddler in a closet while she's having sex on the other side.

Cheryl.

"So while you enjoy your third—" Terence got down from his stool.

"Fourth," she interrupted him, proudly raised it high in cheer, slugged it down.

"In less than an hour, I might add." Terence tsked at her. "I'm going to do a little loop around the place and see who's here tonight."

"Have a nice trip," Guin told him, playfully saluting. She slumped slightly on her stool, willed herself to think of anything, just not Cheryl.

Terence had started off, but backed up a few steps, pointing to a hot blond woman, early thirties, clearly checking Guin out from across the bar. He turned on his sing-song voice, excitedly said, "Someone's looking this way and it's not at me-ee."

"Gotcha, way to keep it on the down-low, Big T." She shook her head at his grade school behavior. "Jesus, this place is such a meat market."

"That's why you come here," Terence said. Then he clapped, looked happy as hell. "Come to think of it, that's why I come here."

"Not anymore, Terence." Tonight she was there to forget— she figured the backdrop of obnoxious club music would just about drown out anything the tequila couldn't kill off.

"Well, looks like Ms. Thang there didn't get the memo." He blasted her with his amazingly cute grin and Guin couldn't help but laugh at him. "Toodles!" he called out, and was gone.

Guin was compelled to look in the direction he'd pointed and immediately made eye contact with the vision of hotness in a too-short skirt. Oh, what the hell. She gave her a little wave. Like a magnet, the woman was at her side. And being the observant nymph she was, she'd sized up Guin's shot in advance and brought over two more.

"A woman bearing gifts of tequila—" Guin playfully placed her hand over her chest, "—is a woman after my own heart."

"Yeah, well, you look like you mean business," the woman said in response to the greeting. She handed her a shot, they clinked glasses. "Same here. I don't like to mess around."

Guin half-smiled, and countered seductively, "You know, I find that very, very hard to believe."

They downed the shots, promptly ordered a couple more.

"I'm Jessie," She introduced herself and plopped her bottom onto the stool next to Guin, nearly giving her a peep show with that miniscule skirt.

"Good to meet you, Jessie. I'm Guin."

"Guin," Jessie repeated. She raised her shot glass high, invited her new friend to do likewise. They clinked glasses for the second time inside only a few minutes. "Here's to new friends, Guin."

It was a cheaper grade tequila and it went down like gravel. Guin quickly sized her up, figured her to be an out-of-towner, buying cheap on someone else's expense account. She'd probably traded her pencil skirt for this micro-mini and came here for a hookup and whatever drinks of better quality someone else would spring for.

"Want to buy me a drink, Guin?"

Bingo. She should be an FBI profiler. The thought had her back on the couch of her house earlier that day, talking with April. April with FBI dreams-turned-LAPD cop. April, making naked guest appearances in her visions…

Christ. She willed the bartender to hurriedly return with the drinks. She was still thinking far too much.

"So, Jessie, I haven't seen you here before." Her inquiry was part cop interrogation, part natural flirtation, and definitely all alcohol induced.

"I live in Vegas. I'm just here on business." More confirmation. And Guin loved the idea of never seeing her again. Jessie was rapidly working her way up to the top of a to-do list Guin didn't even know she had.

A thought suddenly occurred to Guin, causing her to frown a little. "You wouldn't happen to be a lawyer, would you?"

Jessie tossed her head back and laughed uproariously. When she recovered, she asked, "No, why? Do you need one?"

Guin shook her head, smiled. "It's really the very last thing I need, Jessie."

"Good." Jessie nodded, leaned over and whispered loudly over the club music, tickling the inside of Guin's ear. "Because I think I can pretty much cover anything else you need." She rubbed her hand along Guin's thigh, getting dangerously closer to her private property with each teasing pass. "I'd like to show you something."

Jessie jumped down from the stool and took Guin's hand and pulled her through the crowd. Between the throngs of dancers, the booming music, the many drinks and the snaking path they took, Guin's footing was slightly off and she practically bumped head-first into a tough African-American woman. She refused to make eye contact, only excused herself and finished their intended route to the women's restroom. Jessie marched them straight to the front of the line for the handicapped stall, cutting in front of several other couples in line. Guin half-wondered if the stall had ever seen a single wheelchair since it was built. She suspected it had hosted its fair share of couples doing exactly what she was about to do with Jessie.

One couple exited and Jessie stepped in ahead of the others, causing a ruckus on the other side of the door once they were in the stall.

"Hey bitch! Get in line like the rest of us!" someone called from the other side.

Tucked away in her cozy stupor, Guin ignored the rants, enamored with Jessie's business-like approach to ecstasy. The young woman rapidly unzipped and shoved Guin's pants to her ankles, leaned into her and kissed her hard. Guin ran her hand up the woman's bare thigh, beneath her skirt, felt her smooth cheeks there and wondered with delight where Jessie's panties were.

She pulled hard on the woman's blouse, causing a tiny button to pop off and ping against the metal, land somewhere on the floor. She freed one of Jessie's ample breasts from her pretty bra, kneaded it roughly. Jessie reached for her boy briefs, but Guin shoved her hand away.

Guin pressed Jessie against the cool metal. She raised one of Jessie's slender legs, resting her foot on the toilet seat, and then quickly got to work.

"I've gotta fuckin' pee! Dammit!" The voice was still booming on the other side of the door. "Hurry up, for fuck's sake!"

"You like that?" Guin huskily whispered when she felt Jessie practically collapse in her arms. A mere whimper was all she got in response. Guin smiled, pushed herself in further, faster; kissed her harder.

"Hurry the fuck up!" Pounding followed, rattling the stall, helping to mask Jessie's escalating squeals as she reached orgasm. They were breathless, oblivious to the other commotion that had also escalated.

"Come with me back to my hotel room, Guin," she commanded in a heavy breathing whisper.

The request all but ruined the moment. No strings, no hotel, and most importantly, no hotel bed with all its motherfucking, bad-ass karma—Jesus, beds were the worst—a real hot point for her visions. The last thing she needed was an even more disturbing montage of stranger freak-shit while she was in the throes of passion with Jessie-whatever-her-name-was. Guin coldly stepped back, straightened her shirt, fastened and smoothed her pants. She shook her head.

"No, Jessie," she said, mustering all the faux compassion she had within her. "I would, but I came here with a friend. I need to get back to him."

Jessie smoothed her own clothes, looked for the button, quickly gave up on the idea. "Suit yourself. But if you change your mind..." She reapplied her lipstick, made a playful kiss-smack Guin's direction. "Find me."

"Sure thing." Guin smiled, moment over, anxious to go.

Jessie shot her a final sexy glance that would have surely melted a lesser woman. Guin blinked hard, tried not to succumb to her buzzing head, and exited the stall. An exceptionally large woman with a buzz cut was waiting for her there, hands on hips, looking pissed.

"You step in front of me again and you'll have no choice but to use the handicapped bathroom from now on."

"Oh really?" Guin foolishly challenged.

"You done it now. Know what I'm gonna do?" Buzz Cut took a step forward, leered over Guin. "Fuck. You. Up."

The human wall with a buzz cut drew back, prepared to unfurl one powerful blow that promised to deliver a quick, painful end to Guin's night.

"Back off, Charley." The no-nonsense voice came from the other side of the bathroom and its owner emerged from another stall. She coolly strode over to a bank of sinks to wash up, all the while addressing the women involved in the near-scuffle. She held the Buzzcut Giant's stare in the mirror. "Somehow I don't think your parole officer would understand why you were even in a bar in the first place, much less threatening an officer."

Guin finally recognized Jace Sloan. So Sloan was the African-American woman who'd been haunting the bar both times Guin had been there. Suddenly it all made sense. Lieutenant Sloan, from another division of LAPD.

Great.

Charley immediately took a step back, feigned innocence. "I just came in here to use the facilities. The restaurant next door is having a plumbing problem."

"M-hmm," Jace replied warily. She wiped her hands, tossed the towel in the trash, deadpanned, "You better hurry your ass up then. There's a long line waiting."

"I will, thank you."

Amazing how quiet and polite the hulking tower could be. Guin forced an appreciative smile and, given the break, started to make her getaway. Jace gently grabbed Guin's elbow, shook her head.

"Come on. Let's me and you have a little chat."

"Okay."

"And wash your hands first."

Guin did as she was instructed, then obediently followed the woman back into the bar. They took a quiet seat where Jace ordered a beer and a bottle of water. Much to Guin's dismay, the water was for her. She uncapped it, took a swig. The band announced their brief break, and suddenly there was only crowd noise. Guin felt insecure without the cover of drink or obnoxious music.

"I know how much you'd rather help that worm find its way out of the bottle tonight, but I seem to remember you having a job to go to in the morning." Jace took a swig of her own beer, almost taunting Guin with it. She set it down, stared expectantly at the woman across from her.

Guin rolled her eyes. "Well, that worm and me have a deal worked out, so I will be having a couple more shots here to help spring him." She shrugged, started to get down from her stool. "It's fair."

Jace grabbed her elbow again, leaned in closer. "So what exactly do you do in the morning to cover up after a hard night like this one? Hmm?" She let go of her, sat back and took a dainty sip this time. "Your captain must surely notice when you're off. Or is this such a common occurrence that that's all the better he expects out of you?"

Guin regarded her with a blend of guilt and anger. "I give one hundred percent on the job. Never question my dedication to my work again."

"One hundred percent of half-ass is still half-ass."

They were silent for a moment.

Guin softened somewhat, sighed and admitted, "Anyway, Boss starts vacation in the morning."

"I know. Because I'm filling in for him for the rest of this month." Jace glowered at her.

It was a bad night gone worse. Guin wished more than anything that she could strike her unwilling confession from the record.

"But you're not in our division."

"I am now."

"Fuck me," Guin muttered.

"No thank you. You're too busy fucking yourself. And any pretty thing that comes along, apparently." She lowered her chin, arched an eyebrow. "You're reckless."

"This isn't how I normally am," Guin softly defended herself. "I've been going through some…some things."

"I'm aware. Now let's not self-destruct, what do you say." But it really wasn't a question or an offer of comfort. Jace was all business. "You hear what I'm saying?"

"Loud and clear." Guin nodded. She looked at Terence who was standing near the door, scanning the place for her. "Look, I've got to go. There's my ride."

Jace followed her line of sight, clearly relieved that Terence was at the end of it and not some wanton hussy. She nodded.

"I'll expect to see you bright-eyed and bushy-tailed tomorrow, first thing, you hear?"

"Yes, ma'am."

"Or else."

Guin didn't question the woman, only lowered her eyes, and didn't look up again until she was at Terence's side, more than ready for him to deliver her home.

Jace Sloan was right—Guin had no business making deals with worms on work nights.

She was literally spraying her eyes with Visine, willing the redness in her eyes to recede if only a little.

Too much pressure. She'd always juggled priorities—too many classes, too many jobs, too many girlfriends at a time. Throw in internal powers struggling for dominance, the loss of her partner and her two-timing girlfriend, add alcohol and stir. Guin had not only learned to live with chaos, she thrived on it. Until this morning.

She'd slept in, indulged in too long a shower, which had resulted in too little time to get ready. Her curls were wound as tight as she was, her makeup was half-ass, and she could really use some coffee. She'd run out of time waiting for the little two cup pot to brew, had unplugged the thing, and had started out of the kitchen. Had stopped, performed an about-face, and tucked Cheryl's stripes in her uniform pocket just in case.

By the time she reached the station, Guin realized that had Jace Sloan not interrupted her mission of self-destruction the night before, she'd have felt even worse than she did. She simply couldn't imagine it. She was noticeably awkward, slower, and nearly ran smack-dab into April on her way out of the locker room.

"Good morning, sunshine," April said with a playful smile. She sized her partner up. "You look like crap. I take it you went out last night?"

"Yeah." Guin wanted to sneer at her, but there didn't appear to be a trace of malice in April's eyes. She felt compelled to explain herself. "I went out with my buddy, Terence, and had a few drinks. I'll be fine after a little coffee."

"There's fresh stuff in the lounge."

"That sounds good."

April stood there, sweetly grinning. Guin offered her a kind, crooked smile, then side-stepped her. Instead of going into the locker room April followed her.

"How do you like your coffee?" April said, hurrying past her partner. She flicked the nozzle on the coffee urn and filled the tallest cup she could find.

"Uh, black for now."

"Yikes, I said this coffee was fresh, not good." She hunted around for something to put in it. "I like you too much to subject you to this pure tar." She doused the coffee with enough sweetener to make it mildly palatable. She handed it to Guin, waited for her to take a long eye-opening swig.

"So," she asked while Guin caffeinated. "Is there any particular reason why you're torturing yourself this morning?"

"Nothing more than the usual."

April studied her.

"Good morning, ladies." The rich voice came from Detective Clive Burnette. Not wearing his blues this morning, he looked more like a model than a cop in his finely cut Italian suit. Guin snorted softly, smiled over the top of her coffee cup. "Hey, Clive. Nice threads."

"Thank you."

"Have you met my new partner, April?"

April nodded, smiled genially. "Actually, I rode with Detective Burnette for a couple of days before you returned."

Burnette puffed out his chest, shoved his hands in his pockets like a little boy. "I showed her the ropes, introduced her to the area. Piece of cake once you get to know it."

April chuckled. "Well anything's better than East L.A."

Guin was surprised. "You worked East L.A.?"

"Sure did. I still live there."

"Live there?" Another shocker for Guin. "That's a rough place."

Clive refilled his LAPD coffee mug as he listened to the banter.

April smiled, shook her head. "I'm a cop, Guin. I carry a gun."

"That doesn't always matter," Guin said, instantly, if unintentionally, reminding the room about her partner's untimely death.

Clive took a sip, turned serious as if he were paying homage to his fallen comrade. "Yeah, you can never be too careful. That's for sure."

The silence in the room was sudden and thick.

April finally spoke up. "Well, if it makes you both feel better, my lease is up soon and I'm planning on moving closer anyway."

"Good to hear it." Clive patted her back, then added in a macho tone, "East L.A. is no place for somebody like you." He started out the door, called, "You ladies have a great shift."

"Somebody like me?" April repeated in an offended tone, but arched an eyebrow, smiled.

"Yeah, Clive means well." Guin gave her a crooked smile. "He's a goofball."

The detective hurriedly poked his head back in the room. "And April, if you need any help moving, I'll get some guys together, what do you say?"

"Sure thing, Clive. Thanks." April laughed when Clive winked at her. Then he was gone. "He's sweet."

"And he's got a little bit of a crush on you," Guin said between sips. "Can't blame a guy for trying."

April's eyes sparkled mischievously. Guin tried to source out a foreign feeling that tugged at her. One thing she did know for sure, just because she was having erotic visions of her partner was no reason to go soft on her. It was that kind of thinking that caused people to lower their guard, not do their job right, and then bad things happened. Guin bucked up, slugged down the last of the coffee and set her cup in the sink.

April apparently read her partner's sudden change in mood. "You okay?"

"Yeah. Let's go."

Guin continued to basically ignore April as they left the North Hollywood station and rode down Riverside heading toward Vineland. At last the radio interrupted the silence in their squad car. Both women reached for the radio at the same time, but April took command on this one.

"Go ahead."

"Suspicious activity on the ten-thousand block Burbank Boulevard, east of Circus Liquors. Copy?"

"Ten-four. Unit fifty-four responding."

Guin hit the lights and siren. They reached Burbank, reported their location to base and then got out. Unsnapping their holsters as they went, April started ahead of her toward a metal building. Guin grabbed April's shirt sleeve with more force than she'd intended, causing the woman to stop and give her a surprised look.

"No," Guin said. A series of flashbacks of a similar scene more than a month earlier went through her mind and she quickly tamped it down, shook her head. "I'm going ahead, you stay here to call backup."

April's expression relayed both offense and a willingness to follow an order laid out by a more senior officer. She appeared to be deciding whether or not to protest the command, but nodded.

"And cover yourself, for chrissakes," Guin ordered.

Guin edged down the side of the building with her back pressed against it. A loud explosion rocked the building. Flames and smoke burst through the windows. Glass exploded and tinkled to the ground. Guin was knocked to the ground. Just ahead of her, a skeletally thin man burst out of the door and ran like a bat out of hell. Guin quickly recovered, stumbled into a run and made ragged pursuit. She knew a meth lab when she smelled one and could tell a meth addict when she saw one.

Breathless, she rounded the alley, saw a row of dumpsters and the runner who was about to leap up and over to his freedom.

"Stop right there!" she called, nearly keeling from the chase and her hung-over head. "I'll shoot you—believe it."

He raised his hands above his head, cursed under his breath.

After the fire crew taped off the building and the marshal deemed it structurally sound, Detective Burnette rolled into the place and snapped dozens of pictures for evidence. The suspect stood by in cuffs.

April and Guin sat on the bumper of the nearby ambulance filling out paperwork. Burnette called to her as he worked. "You got here just as the place blew?" He made a low whistle, looked at them with a mix of concern and admiration. "You girls could have been seriously hurt."

"Clive, don't call us girls in front of the perp, okay?" Guin didn't look up.

"The lady cop's having a bad day," the young suspect put in with his thick Hispanic accent. A paramedic finished bandaging his forehead and stepped away. "She almost shot me."

Burnette half-smirked, playing along, and nodded in Guin's direction. "Yeah, she's a loose cannon, that one."

"I swear it! She told me she would shoot me because she was having a bad day." Now that he had an audience, the perp grew more boisterous. "I have rights!"

"Shut up," Guin muttered, flipping to a clean page. "Or I'll shoot you right now."

"Geesh, Marcus. You've been uptight since you came back." Burnette gave a demonstrative roll of his shoulders. "You gotta loosen up a little bit. I guess I'd have thought that time off woulda been good for you."

"It wasn't time off. It was mandatory. That's hardly a vacation."

"You got suspended?" the perp nosed.

"Yeah, I shot a meth dealer," Guin deadpanned. She scribbled a tired, illegible signature on the form, closed it, and handed it off to an assisting officer. She looked at the perp. "You're really a piece of shit, you know that?"

"Where do you want him?" April asked.

"I don't care, just not in our car."

"Geesh, lady. You gotta relax," the perp started up again. "You're so angry."

"Shut up," Guin and April said in unison.

"Hold up," Burnette said playfully. "Let me get a picture of that happy bunch."

He aimed his camera at Guin and the perp and snapped a shot. Suddenly Guin was overcome by warmth. It felt the same way as when Cheryl had come to her in the kitchen. She looked around. The feeling faded quickly, and soon she wasn't even sure she'd felt anything in the first place. Burnette fired another flash in her face, effectively bringing her attention back front and center.

"That's enough, Burnette." She looked at April and then at the suspect. "Get him out of here."

Guin stood there long after April hauled him away. Burnette continued to snap the outlying grounds all around her while she waited for her partner to return. "You want me to move?"

"No, ma'am," he told her with a wink. "Just getting extra shots. Your pretty face will be the best thing about these pictures."

Guin rolled her eyes, smirked at her dopey colleague.

CHAPTER TWELVE

After lunch, Detective Burnette laid the evidence pictures out on a lightboard in his office. He carefully matched each marker with the correct shot and made notes. He flipped through the stack until he came to the ones of Guin, April and the perp. Then Guin and the perp. Then Guin…

His eyes grew wide and he held the shot close, studied it for a long time. Without altering his puzzled stare, he picked up the phone and pressed a single button.

"Lieutenant Sloan, Burnette here. I've got those meth lab shots back." He raised the picture to the light, squinted at it before stacking it back with the others. "There's something you should see."

They covered the usual niceties with few words.

"Burnette."

"Lieutenant."

And then Detective Burnette entered her temporary office and shut the door behind him.

"Adjusting?" he politely inquired.

"Trying to." She raised her eyes to him, smiled hospitably enough. "That's why this better be important."

Burnette looked troubled, blinked too much. "It's important. Mostly it's weird."

She made a give-me motion with her hand and he forked over the envelope of crime scene photos. He watched as Jace Sloan carefully examined and shuffled the pictures until she zoomed in on one in particular interest. He patiently awaited her reaction.

There was a very clear image of Sergeant Cheryl Jones standing in the photograph next to Guin. Moreover, Guin appeared to be looking at the woman, and for the first time in as many weeks, she seemed relatively at peace. Cheryl, on the other hand, seemed relatively...transparent.

Sloan stared for several moments, then replaced the photos in the envelope and calmly addressed the detective. "You have a report to accompany this montage?"

He seemed confused. "I do, but..."

"Where is it then?"

"It's on my computer still." He shook his head. "Didn't you see—"

"What I see is an old picture of Sergeant Jones superimposed over top of one of today's crime scene photos." She set it aside. "Technology isn't perfect, Detective."

"But the way Marcus is looking at her..."

"Bring me that report as soon as you're done with it, would you, Detective?"

He stood there, stunned. Lieutenant Sloan looked at him. He shrugged. "Sure."

"Anything else?"

"No, ma'am. There's not." He turned and started to leave her office. "Detective Burnette, are there any more of these?" She nodded toward the envelope he'd just delivered to her.

"Yeah, a few more in that envelope. Some even wackier than that one."

"I see." Lieutenant Sloan seemed to be mulling it over. She reopened the envelope and shuffled through the pictures again. She selected one, studied it for any trace of the apparition and decided it was a clean shot. She handed it to the detective. "That's the one you'll use for this report. Are we clear?"

He took it from her.

"There's no sense in causing a commotion around here over some malfunctioning software. Only makes emotions run high. Gets folks talking nonsense."

"If you say so, Lieutenant."

She looked squarely at the detective, made sure he knew there was no wiggle room on this issue. "I do say so, Detective. I appreciate your cooperation and confidentiality on this matter."

"Of course, ma'am."

"These on your computer?"

"They are." He looked at her blankly, then realized what she was getting at. "You don't want them to be, do you?"

"Take care to delete them, please. And make sure that I have the only disk copy, will you?"

"I will, Lieutenant."

When she was alone again, Jace Sloan took another look at the pictures, laying them out one at a time on her desk. There was no mistaking that the hazy image was Sergeant Cheryl Jones, and she appeared to be interacting with Officer Marcus. Sloan studied them for a long time.

In the lounge, Guin and April were signing off on their daily reports when Sloan poked her head in. She motioned toward Guin.

"Marcus, can I see you in my office, please?" She vanished.

Guin shot April a look.

"You suppose that little weasel drug chef told them I wanted to shoot him?"

April only shrugged. Guin stood up, stretched her arms, eyed the doorway.

"I mean I did want to, but there's protocol to be followed." She heard April's laugh behind her as she went. She followed Sloan at a safe distance and took a seat in front of her desk. Guin noted how very tired she was of being in that chair no matter who invited her to sit in it now. She tried to perk up, look alive.

"Look, if you're going to get on to me again for last night—"

"Marcus, how close were you and Sergeant Jones?"

The question took Guin by complete surprise. Her voice quieted significantly. "Why?"

A knock on the door deferred the answer. Detective Burnette entered. He shot Guin a strange look, handed Sloan a disk.

"As you requested."

"Thank you, Detective."

"Yes, ma'am, is there anything else?"

"No, Detective. But I'll be waiting on your reports."

"Yes, ma'am." He nodded at her, then at Guin. Suddenly he looked sympathetic toward the officer. "Officer Marcus."

With the door shut again, Lieutenant Sloan shoved the disc in her computer and began clicking her mouse. Guin could not see the screen. Sloan absently addressed her as she worked.

"So, is there anything you'd like to share with me?"

"No, Lieutenant. Officer Reese and I were just finishing up our reports from this morning."

"Marcus, I'm referring to my question prior to Detective Burnette's arrival."

"I'm not sure what you want me to say."

Sloan stared her down. "I think you know exactly what I'm talking about, Guin."

Guin leaned back in the chair, tried to look comfortable. There was no way Jace could know the nature of her relationship with Cheryl. Impossible. After she let the lieutenant suffer the silence for a bit, she proffered up a condensed bit of benign information. "Sergeant Jones and I were partners for over three years and we were very close. I knew all of her business and she knew mine. You know how it is when you spend ten hours a day with someone."

Lieutenant Sloan refocused on the screen, on a particular photo of Cheryl reaching a hand out toward Guin.

"Yeah." She ejected the disk, put it in a sleeve and set it inside her desk drawer. Her tone lightened up. "Captain Briggs told me to be sure to spend some extra time with you while he's away. He wanted to make sure you were adjusting okay to your new partner. Is everything going well with you and Officer Reese?"

"Yeah, I think we're going to be a pretty good team."

"That's good to hear, Marcus. Let me know if you ever need to talk."

"Thanks, Lieutenant." She stood, waited for permission to go, and at last Sloan nodded.

She walked down the hallway toward the lounge trying to understand the point of the impromptu meeting. She passed Detective Burnette talking with another officer. Both grew quiet upon her approach and smiled. She felt uncomfortable.

She entered the lounge and quietly stood there, watching April finish up her paperwork. She was getting used to her partner. April was funny, sweet and sexy enough that Guin could definitely see how things could heat up between them; how they could possibly evolve into a relationship. It hadn't been like that with Cheryl. No, her relationship with Cheryl had been a true surprise.

But April seemed to know that Guin found her attractive— or maybe she was used to that kind of attention from all women. And guys, too, Guin privately lamented, recalling Burnette's ridiculous behavior. But it was nice that unlike with Cheryl, Guin and April were equals. It was sort of a sexy balance of power with one very obvious imbalance: Guin knew ahead of the fact that she and April would end up in bed together.

She blinked her eyes, cleared her throat to extinguish the thought. April looked up, granted her a stunning smile.

"Everything okay?"

"Yeah. Just a mental health check." Guin chuckled, twirled her finger around her ear playfully. "Make sure I'm not loco."

"You know what I think?" April clipped the papers together,

snapped them into the clipboard and rose from her seat. She walked toward Guin, quieted her voice. "I think you're all right, Guin Marcus."

The sexily uttered words in conjunction with April's smoky eyes made her feel alive for the first time in more than a month. She felt ripe with need, and wondered—against her own judgment—what process she needed to endure to arrive at that place in her vision; wondered if there was a fast-forward approach. April arched an eyebrow, almost as if issuing her a dare. Then she turned and strode down the hallway in the direction of the locker room. Guin watched her backside as she went, expelled the breath she'd been holding.

On the way home she considered how things had started with Cheryl, beginning with a conversation they'd had in passing, just friends, more than a year ago...

Guin had been forced to break the ice after an overly quiet morning with Cheryl. "What's wrong?" You don't seem like yourself at all today."

Cheryl had shrugged. "I didn't sleep very well last night. Frank and I had an argument and I lost."

"What's that mean?"

"It means he's going hunting next week while I spend my vacation home alone and with kids. We really don't have extra money to do much."

"That doesn't seem fair."

"He justifies it because of my work schedule which he says keeps him from doing what he wants to do." She sighed, rubbed her neck. "I don't even know why I'm married anymore. If it wasn't for the kids..."

"Then you should have something for yourself."

Cheryl looked at her partner, smiled. "I consider the time I'm at work with you to be the highlight of my day most of the time."

Guin laughed. "Wow, you really are deprived."

"Well, we drive and talk, go on some calls, have lunch..." She rolled off the details of a typical day. "Then we talk some more. If you were a guy, you'd be the perfect husband."

Suddenly the urge to kiss Cheryl was overwhelming. Guin

quickly looked away. "Hey, do you wanna go to Henry's and pick up dinner?" Cheryl asked. "Or do you already have plans for after work?"

Guin nodded. "Sure. That's a cheap night."

"Yeah. And then get a drink or something." Cheryl looked as if the idea of a night doing anything without children was an anomaly. She'd wrinkled her nose. "Where do broke people go to get a drink?"

Guin laughed. "Home."

"Well, I don't want to be at my home. That's for sure."

Of course that evening they'd ended up at Guin's house, with Cheryl relaxing on the couch, and Mexican food wrappers and beer bottles all over the coffee table.

Then Cheryl sat up suddenly and put her beer down. "We're still in uniform. And drinking."

"So? We're not on duty." But Cheryl still looked troubled about it. With the comfort of a few beers in her, Guin laughed, peeled off her uniform shirt. "There, better?"

"Pants."

Guin tipped her head, a slow smile growing. "You're kidding, right?"

She stood up and literally dropped her pants around her ankles. Guin stood there in briefs and a tank shirt. "Happy?"

Cheryl laughed hard. Guin only nodded and smirked. "I see how you are. All about the pride of the uniform and there you sit, swilling in the blues. Nice. Hypocrite."

At the challenge, Cheryl too began to strip down. "I hope I'm wearing good underwear," she muttered and quickly checked to be sure. "Shew." She shimmied out of her pants revealing pink boy shorts.

"Nice."

"Really?"

Guin took a step closer to her partner. "Really."

They stood face to face. Guin whispered, "I'm thinking the only thing worse than drinking in uniform is driving the cruiser totally trashed in only your underwear."

Cheryl stared into her eyes. "What now?"

"Call Frank and tell him you're staying here tonight."

"He'll freak," she said. Then she softened. "Let him."

Guin smiled evilly. She stared at her partner, wondered if Cheryl knew what she could be getting herself into. Suddenly she was acutely aware of what she was doing with Cheryl. Married Cheryl, with children.

"You know why we're good partners?" Cheryl interrupted her oddly practical thoughts. She took a step closer. Ran her hand down Guin's thigh. "Because we work well together."

"I'm freaking out a little." Guin muttered the confession.

"Don't." Cheryl leaned over, bridged the last bit of distance between them, and kissed Guin on the neck.

"Whoa, whoa, Cheryl. We can't do this." But Guin's whispered protest wasn't compelling enough to cause her partner to stop. Guin chuckled and Cheryl issued her a look that demanded she explain her laughter. "It's actually not funny. Not you anyway—it's just that you're the straight one and I'm the one who's playing hard to get. And oh boy, this is so not what I'm used to."

Cheryl quickly took a step back. Her voice raised in pitch. "Oh, my God. You're not interested."

"I can assure that's not it." Guin raked her hand through her hair, sighed, stammered, "You're married. With kids—"

"Guin," Cheryl cut her off. "I've done this before."

It was a revelation more stunning than the fact that they were in their skivvies in Guin's living room. "No shit?" she softly said.

Cheryl smiled shyly, nodded. "It's on me. So if you want to kiss me back, I'd really like it. But if you don't then we'll just go back to the way things were."

Guin looked contemplative for several seconds. "I wonder if this could be considered sexual harassment."

It was the last thing Cheryl expected. Guin cracked a smile. She pulled Cheryl toward her.

Cheryl smiled. "For that, you better kiss me."

Guin only hesitated a moment longer before she arrived at a mental "all in" declaration. She reached behind Cheryl's back, unfastened her bra with one move and kissed her neck, working a trail upward.

Their first mutual kiss was long and hard. Then off came the scant remaining clothing between them and there was no turning back. They made love several times, until the early morning hours when Cheryl left to go home. Marital insurance, she'd called it.

The next day, Cheryl had pulled up in the cruiser like usual to pick up Guin for work.

During that silent ride, Guin at last asked the obvious question. "Are you mad at me about something?"

"I didn't sleep well last night."

"Look if you're feeling weird or guilty…"

"No." she pulled the car to a stop at the light. They sat in silence until it turned green. At last Cheryl whispered with true hurt in her voice, "Frank didn't even notice I'd come home."

"I'm sorry." Guin mumbled. "I really am."

They rode in silence a few more blocks. When they reached the station parking lot, Cheryl suddenly turned to Guin. "So, what are you doing Monday night?"

Guin hesitated before responding in a quiet, playful, yet questioning tone. "I think I'll be with a very attractive brunette."

Cheryl's smile lit up the car.

And for a year they'd dodged Beth and Frank and anyone close to them and indulged in many, many extended lunches.

CHAPTER THIRTEEN

April would not rest until she'd convinced Guin to get a drink with her after work. Guin ultimately caved only to avoid being rude. The bar they chose was only blocks from her own apartment. They traded their uniforms for track suits from Guin's locker, one of which had fit April just fine.

"This is genius," April said, thumbing the zip-up jacket.

"Yeah, I always keep a few stashed at work. Can't drink in uniform blues." Guin's eyes lit up as the bartender slid two tequilas in front of them. She chuckled. "Everyone thinks I'm such a dedicated runner."

"Oh come on, you're a runner." It was clearly a compliment. April eyed the amber liquid in the shot glasses. She gave it a sniff, continued, "Where do you run?"

"Mostly to the bar," came Guin's monotone answer. She

raised her shot, waited for April to do the same. "A salute to Australia."

"Salute," April chimed in. They clinked tiny glasses and tossed back the shots. Guin pushed her glass forward, indicating she was ready for another. April grimaced, even panted. "Was that tequila? Goes down like gasoline."

"Two more gasolines, please," Guin directed the nearby bartender, without missing a beat.

"Yikes." April was still cringing when the second round came. "I'm glad I could convince you to get a drink with me, no matter how horrendous your choice of beverage."

"Yeah, well I guess since I'm stuck with you I might as well make the best of it." Guin didn't laugh, and April eyed her warily as they clinked glasses a second time. They slugged down two more of the shots.

April slammed the shot glass down, nearly spat. "Christ, how do you drink this stuff?" She grabbed a lime wedge.

Guin tried to hide a grin.

"You think this is funny?"

"No." But the word was wrapped inside a laugh. Guin amended her answer, "Maybe a little."

"You're really a brat, aren't you?" April gently chastised her. She smiled, nodded. "Yeah, a total brat. I thought so."

April motioned to the bartender for water and nearly drained the glass in one long drink. She wiped her lips on a cocktail napkin.

"Oh, I found a place. It's on Chandler."

Guin wriggled her eyebrows. "On Chandler, huh? La-di-da."

"Well, the low-rent side of Chandler." She drank more water.

"So, when you moving in?"

"I get the keys next week and until then I'll spend my every spare moment packing." She grinned. "So this little outing is my last hurrah before I'm too tired to ever move a muscle again."

The bartender was hovering near them and Guin gave him a nod. "Well, then we better make it worth your while. If you want me to help with the move, I can."

"Really?"

"Sure." Guin nodded. "If it's good enough for Burnette, it's good enough for me."

"Thanks, I appreciate that." The bartender delivered fresh shots and April slid one toward her partner. They raised glasses for another toast. "Considering I didn't think you liked me when we first met."

"I didn't," Guin said and downed her shot. April's jaw was slightly gaping. Guin quickly smiled, allaying her partner's fear that she was serious. "No offense. I just wasn't ready to say hello to a new partner when I wasn't done saying goodbye to my old one."

"I get it. No offense taken." April looked earnest, then injected a little silliness. "Especially if you're going to lug my crap across town."

A rugged looking cowboy type—boots and all—sauntered into the bar and hoisted himself onto a stool down a ways. He gave a nod their way, probably directed at April. Guin suddenly felt slighted.

The cowboy ordered a Budweiser, glanced their way a second time, clearly flirting with April.

"Take a look at that," April said. She nudged Guin his direction. As if she could miss him.

"Sorry, not my type. He's all yours."

"My type?" came April's shocked-sounding whispered reply. "No way. You kidding me?"

"Well then, what kind of guy do you go for?"

April's expression was a hybrid of offense and humor. "The kind that are girls, as if you had to ask."

Guin should have figured as much, thanks to her visions. Though it had crossed her mind that April might become a convert or dabbler, like Cheryl had been. Or worse, maybe April knew about Guin's visions. Maybe she was a mind reader. Far be it from Guin to discount such abilities, given her own. All these things conspired in her head, and manifested into a strange expression.

"Oh, come on," April said, looking at her incredulously. "That's all the better your gay radar is?"

Guin snapped out of her daze, struck by the accent-garbled phrase. "You mean, gaydar?"

"Whatever," she said, somewhat flustered. "But seriously, you couldn't tell?"

Guin gave her a quick, embarrassed once-over. "Well, not by looking at you, if that's what you mean."

"What else would I mean? I could tell it about you right away," April said smugly.

It had turned into an absurd conversation. "Oh really?"

"In fact, it crossed my mind that that's why Captain Briggs paired us up."

Growing more absurd by the second...

"What?" Guin laughed to break her own mounting tension. "You think he was matching up the two lezzies?"

"You mean there's only the two of us?"

Guin's chuckle died as she thought about Cheryl again. Her former partner's naked body pressed up against hers, their legs intertwined under covers, the feel of her soft lips as they kissed...

"Guin?"

"No, I don't think Briggs would do that." Or would he? After all, he had to have known that something was going on between her and Cheryl. But there was department policy that forbade such things. Then again there was a matter of her own mental health. She was a bit of a loose cannon, as Burnette had teased— perhaps giving her a hot partner was a sort of insurance that she would continue to report to work? Boy, that would certainly be something the LAPD's HMO didn't cover...

Insanity. She shrugged it off.

"Earth to Guin." April waved her hand before her partner's face. "Hello? Where did you go?"

Guin blinked. "I was just... thinking."

"Okay." April glanced at her watch, sighed. "Well, I need to sober up a bit before driving all the way back. Wanna grab a bite?"

"Sure." Guin set a couple of bucks tip on the bar top. "Do you like sushi?"

"I love sushi."

"Good. I know a place near here."

They noticed the cowboy still watching them.

April shuddered. "Maybe we should go to the ladies' bar next time."

Feeling a new wave of self-confidence given April's fresh confession, Guin only shook her head. "Nah, he's harmless." But she glanced over in time to see Cowboy shoot them a wink. She hopped down from her stool. "Well, on second thought..."

April nodded. "Yeah."

After dinner and the long drive back to her place, April was surprised to see a late-model Benz parked in her designated space. She sighed. A nearby guest spot was vacant and she pulled into it and locked her car. The security lights had been broken for weeks and despite her repeated reminders to the super, the lot was pitch-black. She wedged her keys between her knuckles and headed for the building. In this neighborhood, one always had to be prepared. She waved her fob before the electronic security eye and was granted entry. Once inside she was met with yet another surprise.

"What in the hell are you doing here?"

A pale, Twiggy-thin woman sat cross-legged on the floor in front of her apartment door, eyes closed, leaning against the wall as if she'd been napping there.

"Hello to you, too," the woman sleepily remarked as she came around. "I wondered if you'd recognize me these days."

"I always recognize trouble." April didn't smile, just jammed her key into the door lock and pushed past the woman. She sighed, stepped back and made an obligatory wave toward her apartment. What else could she do? "Come in, Lauren."

"Can you help me up?" Lauren's voice sounded particularly weak. Always the damsel in distress, April knew better.

"Jesus, you're white as a sheet. What'd you bring me? A plague?" April was fed up in advance with whatever tactics her guest would surely try to inflict upon her. She extended her hand and pulled the frail figure off the floor. "Didn't your mom ever tell you to stay home when you're sick?"

Lauren followed her into the apartment. She lugged an oversized gold leather purse over trendy black leggings and long striped tunic. Altogether it looked more like a tent than a fashion statement. No matter, April was sure it was the best style money could buy. She rolled her eyes.

"I need to talk to you." Lauren plopped down onto the couch. Started to slip off her designer boots, but April raised a hand to halt her from getting too comfy.

"I think it's a little late to talk now. I don't have time for this." April dropped her gym bag on the countertop, turned to assess her former lover. Lauren's hair was pulled into a simple straight ponytail revealing perfect streaks of blond highlights in her auburn hair and further emphasizing her pale, pointy cheekbones. "And I mean it—whatever diet you're trying is wretched. You truly look terrible."

"Thanks. Great to see you, too."

April grabbed a water out of the fridge, half-heartedly offered one to Lauren who declined. She sat on a bar stool across the room from her, took a swig, prepared her defenses.

"So, what's so urgent that you needed to come here, park in my assigned space with what I'm assuming is her car? Couldn't we do this over the phone?" April's voice was quickly ramping up in anger.

"I needed to see you in person."

"How did you manage to get in my building anyway?"

"Same thing I did before. I told the landlady I'm your sister."

April folded her arms, pulling Guin's track suit jacket more tightly around her body, as if to glean a little bit of needed emotional strength from it. "All right. So talk."

"I want to come back."

April dropped her arms, felt her jaw fall in surprise. "What? Are you kidding me?"

"Look—Lisa and I broke up. She left me her car, all right. And also three months of unpaid rent and a stack of bills." She rubbed at the worry lines that coursed across her forehead. Her big finish was a whisper, "Landlord locked me out of the apartment. Here I am."

April looked at Lauren with sheer disbelief. At one time she would have done anything for this woman. "So, you just want to…move right into here? With me?"

"I don't have anywhere else to go. Please, April."

April felt her anger peak. She took several deep breaths, tried to be reasonable. Her response was brief and to the point. "You broke my heart."

"I know it. And I'm sorry." Lauren stared at her boots. Everything about her at that moment was pathetic. But even in that state, the poor-little-rich girl was not willing to own even the smallest part of her actions as she added, "I'm sure I don't have to tell you how erratic your hours are."

"Yeah, well it's called earning a living," she snapped back. "I promise you most of the people in this world can attest to that. Most of us were not born with the benefit of a trust fund."

Lauren's head bobbed close to her chest as she sighed.

April studied her for a moment, stated her conclusion. "And it doesn't take a rocket scientist to know that if you're here, something's wrong." She paused a beat, got no reaction. "They cut you off, didn't they?"

Lauren nodded. She raised her eyes to her ex at last. "I still love you."

April hadn't seen that coming. She wondered if Lauren had confused love and need. Being needy was surely a foreign concept for the young woman.

"Sorry, I can't do that." But her words lacked the strength she would have preferred. She hopped off the stool. "I'm just getting my life back together. And I'm not staying here anyway. My lease is up and I'm moving at the end of the month."

Lauren could have guessed that from the few boxes already scattered around the place. Her voice grew significantly quiet. "Where to?"

"I've been transferred to North Hollywood and I've found a place in the Valley." She took the last swig of her water and dropped it into the recycling container, then confidently announced, "I'm moving on, Lauren."

That rejection hit home for real was evident in Lauren's eyes. At last she stood, gathered the bag that was bigger than her, forced a smile. "Fair enough. I lose."

April followed her to the door. Lauren stopped once more. Her eyes were unnaturally large, sunken in appearance.

"Maybe you can let me know when you get settled." Lauren waved her hand slightly. "Maybe we can go for a drink or something."

"Maybe," April said. Once the door was closed and locked, she leaned against it, breathed a sigh of relief. She was getting stronger. Still, there was no reason to tempt herself unnecessarily.

"Or maybe not."

CHAPTER FOURTEEN

A stretch of Ventura Boulevard that bordered Studio City housed Vivica's, one of the best breakfast joints in the state, as far as Guin was concerned, possibly even the planet. It was the perfect place to kick off the weekend. The patronage was a mixture of starlets and everyday folks lurking behind sunglasses, hoping to be mistaken for starlets. Tables lined the patio where waiters served up Frisbee-sized pancakes and cups of coffee that outshined any national chain.

Terence watched Guin wolf down her breakfast. She felt his stare, stopped her fork in midair.

"What is it?" She set the fork down, hesitantly touched her nose. "Boog?"

"No boog." A smile emerged on his face. "This is nice—I mean a little barbaric, but nice."

"What?" she asked between bites.

"Seeing you eat again. Enjoying food." He reassessed her shoveling. "Sort of, anyway."

"I know," she said, blotted her lips, sipped her orange juice. "I'm starting to get back to normal. Well, normal for me anyway. Feels pretty good."

"Good." He had left his own breakfast untouched. He clasped his hands, leaned forward slightly toward her. "So does this mean that you and your new partner are getting on well?"

Guin arched an eyebrow. "We're not getting it on."

"That's not what I said. You know it." Terence playfully punctuated his words with his fork. "Well? Things are good?"

Guin seemed to consider it. "Yeah, she's okay, that one."

"And the porno future flashes?"

Guin nearly choked, covered her mouth with her napkin and swallowed carefully.

"Would you stop it?" She glanced around her. Guin took another sip, cleared her throat. "No, but she's pretty cool to hang out with. Pretty...open-minded."

"Well, we kinda already know that from the previews." Terence joked.

"Very funny. I'm talking more about maybe being able to share other information with her."

"Oh my God. Are you going to tell her about your powers?" Terence's surprise response boomed loudly, alerting the folks in the immediate vicinity. Guin shot him a death ray look, shushed him. A man with distinct features at the next table seemed to tune them in. He looked familiar, like a character actor. Or maybe it was just because of all the lines on his face, Guin couldn't be sure.

She leaned in close. "I'm thinking about it."

Terence lowered his tone. "You think she'll be okay with it?"

"Either that or she'll think I'm crazy. I mean there's really only two ways to go with it, you know?"

Terence looked thoughtful as he scooted scrambled eggs around his plate. "Just be careful, Guin. You have to work with her and you never know how people are going to react to...it."

"Nothing I haven't already thought of." She rolled her eyes. "The last thing I need is another leave of absence." Thoughts of termination, even men in white coats flitted through her brain. She added, "Or worse."

"Well, play it by ear. Maybe the right circumstances will present themselves and it won't be as much of a shock."

Guin turned her attention back to her plate and swallowed a mouthful of pancakes. "What kind of circumstances could possibly make news like that any less weird."

"You're right. It's not exactly natural," he agreed. As an afterthought he smiled, his eyes gleamed mischievously as if he couldn't help himself, as he added, "Supernatural, maybe."

"Funny." Guin waved her fork like a wand, changed the subject. "What about you? Any prospects these days?"

"No. Working too much to get involved. You know how it is," Terence said with zero conviction. It meant there was someone, but he wasn't ready to talk about him yet.

"Sure. So, what's his name, wise guy?" She could tell he was trying to determine what he'd done to summon up that information. She rolled her eyes. "It wasn't a vision, it was your face. You have no idea how to be coy. So bad at it."

"I don't know what you're talking about." His face grew redder.

"Oh yeah, you're getting some."

Now it was Terence's turn to shush her. He glanced around nervously. "Keep it down."

"So, what's his name?" She pushed her plate aside, gave him her undivided attention. "I'm all ears."

"Only because you ate everything but the flatware." He made an exasperated sigh. "I'm not ready to talk about him yet."

"Bullshit. You tell me everything." She shrugged. "I tell you everything."

"I'm trying to pace myself with Mark."

"Mark?" Her face lit up. She pretended to swoon, patted her heart. "His name is Mark."

"Guin!" It was an angry whisper.

"Fine. Sorry." She picked up her juice glass, took a sip. "I'll wait until you're ready."

"Thank you."

She attempted to guilt him. "Though I tell you all of my stuff."

"Guin…"

"Or maybe I should just touch this fork and pick up some energy…" She tiptoed her fingers across the table causing Terence to swipe his utensils out of the way so quickly that the knife fell and clattered loudly on the patio. Guin burst out laughing, clapped.

"You are back to normal," he scoffed. "A normal brat."

She burst into a smile that only lasted a moment. Her attention was suddenly focused over Terence's shoulder. Terence turned around to see a familiar-looking woman, mid-fifties, escorted by a significantly younger man. The woman spotted the pair, immediately waved and headed their direction.

"Fuck me twice on Sunday," Guin muttered under her breath. The woman reached their table in seconds.

"Guinevere," she cooed in a phony, sing-song voice.

Guin lowered her eyes, spoke through a clenched smile. "Mother."

She was aware that Terence's eyes were saucer-wide. He'd only seen a single crinkled picture of Guin's nightmarish mother, Gloria, and now here she was, in the Botoxed flesh.

"That's all you've got for your mother?" the woman asked. Her cheerful tone harbored a sharp edge. Gloria stood there in all her designer glory, her enhanced cleavage bursting out of her ridiculously tight flowery dress. A floppy hat protected her perfect blond hair from the sun, its wide brim purposefully drooping over one eye. It was quite a picture. Gloria thrust her cheek forward, as if Guin would rise up and kiss her hello. The move served to "accidentally" further emphasize her breasts. When Guin ignored the action, Gloria bent down, placing her cheek even closer. Again she was ignored. Gloria gave up and stood up.

"Who's your young man?" She regarded Terence like a starving dog might regard a steak.

"I'm Terence." He stood briefly, shook her hand and re-seated himself in accordance with the warning glare Guin was issuing him.

"Terence is a friend of mine," she tersely stated.

"I see that." Gloria's smile was intended to convey her hope that perhaps he was something more. "I'm very, very happy to see that."

"I'm still a gay homosexual lesbian queer, Mother." Guin's voice conveyed the sharp-toned emotion of a never-ending sore spot.

Guin could have slapped her mother with less impact. An older gentleman at the next table stifled a chuckle. Gloria's date didn't so much as wince; clearly he'd been instructed not to, such was the role for eye candy. But Gloria's face burned an angry shade of red.

"There's no need to be rude about it."

Guin shrugged, forced a false smile. "Since when is telling the truth rude?"

When it appeared that her mother was looking around for a few spare chairs to join them, Guin pushed her own chair back and stood up and slapped a twenty on the table. "You can have this table. Terence and I were just leaving."

She pulled Terence's arm, trying not to notice that he was hurriedly grabbing the still-untouched bacon and muffin off his plate as she dragged him away.

In the parking lot she let out the tiniest growl of exasperation. "What a nutty bitch."

"That's no way to talk to me," Terence chastised her. "I just left my entire breakfast for you, after all."

She leaned onto her car roof, stared at him. A slow-growing smile appeared on her face. "Welcome to the family that puts the fun in dysfunctional."

She popped the locks and they got in and drove back toward their end of the Valley.

"At the risk of pissing you off, she really wasn't as bad as I thought she'd be. Of course your little comment didn't help matters much."

"You kidding?" Guin shot him a look. "My 'little comment' is who I am. She was only acting decent in the first place because she was with a new man. She's not going to go all *Mommy Dearest* on me with him around. I had to call her out. Couldn't help myself."

"So much drama." He sighed, stuffed the last bit of muffin in his mouth, spit little crumbs into the air as he went on. "Reminds me of my own father."

Guin hit the brakes at the stoplight, squinted at him. "Your father's nothing like that at all. Your father's a drag queen. How can he possibly remind you of her?"

"I think it was the dress." He sighed. "God, Dad loves Halston."

She locked gazes with him until the light changed and he motioned for her to go. They rode in silence.

Terrence reached across the seat and squeezed her hand. "You're a good girl, Guin."

She nodded, but felt as if every moment she were sliding dangerously close to her own undoing.

CHAPTER FIFTEEN

The funky breakfast and appearance by Gloria wasn't an ideal initiation for her two day-off cycle. By evening of day one, Guin was still sulking and contemplating going into full shut-down mode, holing up with a bottle of tequila, blinds drawn, phone off.

Instead, she surprised herself by throwing on sweats and heading for the gym. As if it wasn't of her own will, she simply floated along, obeying something that told her drinking two nights in a row would require more than just a two day-off cycle to recover.

The beauty of her favorite workout was that she could imagine the bag bearing Gloria's over-plumped lips and tight brow, and kick, box and otherwise beat the hell out of the thing. It was strangely therapeutic.

By the end of her days off, she was fresh. And sober. Not just sobering up. "Hello you," April said with a grin the next morning as they drove to their first call. "You look totally reset. How are you?"

Guin gave her a genuine smile, nodded. "I feel good."

"Do anything exciting the last few days?"

"Not really." She felt remarkable pride about that admission. It wasn't perfect, but it was a start. "Not really much at all."

They arrived at the scene at a family-owned construction company in North Hollywood where a theft had been reported. April jumped in, interviewed Mike Bateman, the owner.

"Fools cut right through the chain links." He waved at the heavy gate.

April made a note. "Did they take anything else besides the Bobcat?"

"Nope, just my expensive tractor." He looked genuinely befuddled. "We've been in this neighborhood for twenty-two years with a good reputation. Who would steal a brand-new tractor from us?"

Guin left them and took a look around. Sure enough, the remnants of a chain lay in a heap on the ground. It had clear cut marks, and Guin knelt to examine it.

"Bolt cutters, industrial strength, judging by the quick, clean marks." She recited the information for April's notes. She snapped several pictures. "I'm going to collect the links and maybe we can match the tool marks in the system."

April jotted it down. She turned back to Mr. Bateman. "Sir, do you have an alarm system on the property?"

"Have to for insurance, not that we ever needed it before." He nodded toward the small building a few yards away. "For some reason the damned thing didn't go off. When I get a hold of Valley Alarm Company, I'm gonna—"

"I know this is frustrating for you. We're trying to do everything we can to—"

"To what?" Bateman interrupted her sweet reassurance. "To make sure it doesn't happen again? I never see any police down this road unless they're stopping across the street for coffee. My tax dollars at work—that's what I get?"

"I understand how you must feel."

Guin overheard April's patient response, admired it. She herself didn't do well with hopping-mad people. She continued down the chain-link fence, snapping pictures of the hedges there. Sunlight glinted off metal, caught her attention. She knelt down and separated the hedge.

"Never mind the tool marks. Found 'em," she softly called. She snapped on a pair of latex gloves and carefully fished the bolt cutters out of the brush, trying to protect any fingerprints.

"Son of a bitch!" And the owner was on a rant again. His words, loud as they were, faded into the background as Guin was hit with a burst of energy that effectively transported her to the crime scene as good as if she'd been there.

She smelled diesel fuel, and saw a man wearing all black pushing the Bobcat up a makeshift ramp and onto a trailer. Silver pickup truck. No faces. Soft talking. Sounds of crickets. The truck fired up with a throaty rumble and she wondered how anyone could say they'd heard nothing.

She was acutely aware that she should be doing something—not like she could stop the perps inside a vision. The license plates! She ran toward the truck. It spun out, creating a soft flurry of gravel dust. Then it was gone.

"Dammit!" she said softly, but with conviction. She opened her eyes and realized that April had come to stand next to her. Her partner's forehead was creased with worry.

April tipped her head inquisitively. "Guin? You okay?"

Guin stared at her a moment, blinked, then nodded. She stammered, concocting a command performance fib. "I...just realized I don't have anything to bag these up."

"I've got paper in the car." But April didn't budge. "You sure you're okay?"

Guin nodded. "I'm good."

A radio call interrupted any further friendly interrogation.

"Another robbery?" April wrinkled her nose. "This day isn't going to let up."

"Oh yeah?" Guin absently remarked, still shaking off the vision.

"At this rate? I don't have to be a psychic to see that." April tore off a copy of the report, tucked the rest into the clipboard box. "Not that I believe in that hocus-pocus."

Guin blinked, felt compelled to respond lest she look suspicious. "Right."

April started away, but stopped short, backed up a step. "You sure you're okay?"

"Yeah. I'm good." Guin's second effort at reassuring her was more believable. She hung back a moment, watched as April headed for the cruiser. A chill reverberated throughout her body. She shrugged it off, muttered, "Hocus-pocus…?"

The second call took them only blocks away to a production rental facility. They strode up a cement walkway, passed a metal sign, Protected by Valley Alarm Company.

April noticed it too, remarked, "Lotta help they were last night."

"They've got pretty much all the business in the Valley." Guin held the gate open for April to enter. "Never had any complaints before."

They went straight to the large metal building where the door had been obviously pried open. Guin ran a gloved hand along the marred doorjamb. Her visionary reaction was as strong as rubbing a genie out of a bottle: Two guys exiting the premises, lugging expensive camera equipment and what looked like DVD players, a television. It was dark, and she stood there watching the burglars traipse right past her, gear in hand, making their getaway. She was helpless to stop them.

Guin drew her hand back as if she'd touched fire. She checked to see that April hadn't witnessed her spell, but her partner was busy sorting through the building and snapping pictures. Guin took a deep breath. These new sensations were strong, perhaps because the crime was fresh. And when she emerged from the spontaneous bursts of imagery, she couldn't be sure how long she'd been "gone." Nervous sweat beaded on her forehead.

The manager joined them.

"Thanks for coming out, officers. I'm Bob Crayton, half owner," he politely addressed them, and offered his handshake. Guin reluctantly reciprocated, leery of touching anything at this point. But the old guy's touch emanated truthfulness, immediately putting her at ease. He continued, "Never had anything like this happen before."

"I have on my record that you had officers out here a few times last year," Guin countered, jotting notes on her clipboard.

"Tagging and a little vandalism," he confessed. "Couple of middle school kids. I didn't want to get 'em in trouble, but I had to file the report to get insurance to pay for the sandblasting to remove the paint. That's a chore."

"I see." Guin looked around for her partner; she was headed their way, department camera bouncing around her neck, cushioned by her breasts. Guin sighed, looked anywhere else. She turned back to the owner. "We'll drop by a copy of this report this afternoon, would that be okay, Mr. Crayton? Should satisfy the insurance company."

"Sure." He gave a cursory look around. "I guess it's no wonder they hit this place. All these electronics? Stuff will probably surface on eBay next week."

"We have a sting operation that looks for that stuff," Guin told him. "Any serial numbers would be helpful in identifying your property if we recover it."

"I've got them in a file inside." He nodded. "Otherwise, I left everything exactly as it was. Didn't touch a thing. Just called you guys—er, ladies."

April shook her head. "Do you have a list of missing items, Mr. Crayton?"

"I've counted three HD cameras because they were scheduled for loan out starting tomorrow." He shook his head, looked disgusted, but maintained his kind demeanor. "I think that's probably about it."

"And some DVD players and a monitor." Guin was narrating her vision before she could stop herself. She suddenly had two very attentive sets of eyes trained on her. She shrugged, stammered, "It was, uh, written on the empty boxes."

April looked behind them, then back to Guin. Unwilling to dismiss it so easily, she left them at the doorway and poked back through the inventory. Guin held her breath as April dug through the boxes. She selected one, held it high and turned it upside down to show that it was empty.

"Monitor," she read the miniscule description typed on the box label. She looked curiously at her partner. Guin swallowed hard, wondered how she was going to explain her way out of that one. April burst into a smile. "Girl, you've got eagle eyes."

The old guy chuckled, so did April. Guin laughed last, thankful for the diversion.

"There's been another break-in not far from here." April told him, coming back to join them. "We'll treat the cases with the thought they could be related."

"Let me know what you come up with." He looked at his watch. "I have to get back into the office. My buddy's down with the flu. We're a two-man operation here."

"I understand," April said, smiling sweetly. "We'll be in touch, Mr. Crayton."

Back in the cruiser, Guin nervously hoped her partner wouldn't badger her about her Superman-worthy eyesight. She suddenly remembered that she hadn't inquired about April's weekend and went there to head off inquiry. "You get your stuff all packed up?"

The memory of it prompted a tired sigh from April. "Yes, thank God." She drummed her thumb on the steering wheel. "I can't wait to put that place behind me."

Guin got the very distinct impression that there was more than an apartment she was eager to leave, but she didn't ask and April didn't elaborate.

"Well, good," Guin said, concentrating on anything else. The last thing she wanted was to be picking up more energy than she already had from April. Perhaps her preoccupation with her previous visions about the two of them together was what caused her verbal negligence when she heard herself say, "It'll be nice to have you closer."

Her words hung thickly, like a mysterious fog inside the patrol car. It was an inadvertent admission, and Guin didn't dare move to recover from it at the risk of accidentally overqualifying her statement. If April recognized this, she must have merely perceived it as a positive step in her favor, and the conversation turned to genial chatter the rest of the way back to the station.

But the afterglow of the statement lingered, and the visions of her and April were ever-present in Guin's mind. She was past her initial shock and was treading apprehensively, sometimes fearfully in deep waters. Simple enough—there would be a time when their relationship would go to the next level, and knowing this in advance of their casual friendship was…weird.

The fearfulness came with realizing how careless she'd been the last time; emotions conspired to upset concentration, and in her line of duty, concentration was the difference between a good bust and having your dead partner's blood on your hands. Literally.

"Well, I hope your offer still stands to help me move." April shot her a hopeful grin. "We'll have Clive and one of his friends for the heavy stuff."

"Clive, shmive." Guin pretended to scoff. "You have seriously underestimated my superhuman strength."

"Well, you've got superhuman eyesight, that's for sure."

"Well, I'll be there." Guin hurriedly put them back on track.

"Thanks. I appreciate it." April patted Guin's leg, setting off a tingle under her uniform. She sat stone-still, swallowed hard, looked out the window. A fifteen-year-old boy would have exploded under similar circumstance.

"Possible four-fifteen at 2364 Riverside Drive, Valley Alarm Company. Unit fifty-four please respond."

Guin pressed the button. "Ten-four. Unit fifty-four responding."

The partners turned to face each other, said in unison, "Mike Bateman."

April sighed, pulled a quick U-turn and hit the lights and siren.

CHAPTER SIXTEEN

As expected, Mike Bateman was creating a scene at Valley Alarm when they arrived.

"I pay my bill every month, have quarterly inspections! I set that damned alarm every night myself!"

"Sir, you'll have to calm down." It was Ted the manager, according to his name badge. He was older, bearded, thick glasses magnifying his brightened blue eyes. He aimed his pleading eyes toward Guin and April. "Officers, please?"

Since she'd been able to calm him once already that day, April made her way to the irate customer a second time.

"Mr. Bateman, I know this is what you feel like doing, but you have to let us handle it. I'd hate to see you get into trouble because you're angry."

"Lady, I've got a five thousand dollar deductible. With

business slow, I don't have five thousand clams burning a hole in my pocket!"

Guin blew out a tired breath. April had been right, it didn't take a psychic to see that it was going to be a long, long day.

"I tried to tell him," Ted explained, a tone of real desperation in his voice. He explained it like a seasoned salesman. "The battery backup would kick on in the event of a power failure. And in the event of low battery life, it beeps—loud. There's no way this alarm malfunctioned. It could only be human error."

"Bullshit!" Bateman had overheard the white-haired guy explaining things to Guin. "I follow those instructions to the letter, every night."

"Impossible!" Ted burst out. His face looked even redder given the contrast of his bushy white eyebrows. "Look, I'm not trying to rip anybody off. I'm in the business of not ripping people off!"

"Says you!"

"All right, all right!" Guin couldn't get their attention. She pressed her fingers into the corners of her mouth, let loose a shrill whistle that probably started dogs barking in a four-block radius. At last she had all eyes on her. "Thank you. Okay now, let's everybody calm down."

"I'm Ted Johnston." The gentleman extended his hand, and ever begrudgingly, Guin was again forced to touch someone. "I was doing the books and Mr. Bateman came in here raving about his system! What can I do about it?" His voice rose.

Guin made a downward motion with her hand. "Let's use our indoor voices, Mr. Johnston. Now, Officer Reese and I responded to the call at Mr. Bateman's construction company this morning, so I understand how he may be a little upset with your company right now."

"Upset?" Bateman took a single stride across the room, too close to the old guy for Guin's comfort. "I just lost a brand-new Bobcat, and this fool is telling me that we're to blame for that?"

"Ninety-six-point-two percent of all alarm failures are actual human failures." The man sounded like a statistician.

"Hang on, fellas," April said in a calming tone. "We're going to take down a report and call it a day on this. Then, when nerves have been restored and tempers are down, you can resolve this civilly."

"And if you can't, you can resolve it in civil court..." Guin whipped out a fresh report sheet and sighed. She'd be up to her ass in paperwork for the rest of the day at this rate.

"Agreed?" April's eyes flitted between the men. "Agreed?" she said more loudly. They both nodded.

Guin looked around for a flat surface to write on.

"You can use that computer desk over there. It used to be the secretary's before the budget cuts."

"Probably because of your stinking alarm systems," Bateman put in just to show that he wasn't afraid to do so, even in the presence of the law. Guin shot him a look and sat down.

The cool metal chair chilled her through her uniform pants and immediately a vision unwound itself in her tired head.

He'd sat at this desk. In front of this computer. He, he, he...who was he? She stood over his shoulder; saw wispy ends of blond hair poking from beneath a ball cap. He checked over his shoulder nervously and so many times, Guin had an absurd notion to duck. He did not see her. The keyboard clacked beneath his smooth strokes and line after line appeared on the screen before him.

Codes.

Guin blinked hard, realized she was staring at a ball cap perched upon an antique typewriter. Faded words read Shelby's Mustang Diner. She absently touched it. He'd worn it. The blond boy.

Suddenly there was a hand on her shoulder and Guin leapt out of her seat. She stood breathless in front of Bateman.

"I'm sorry, what?"

Everyone stared at her. April took a step closer. Guin wondered how long she'd been gone again.

Bateman appeared almost as startled as she was. He lowered his voice; spoke in the most polite tone he'd utilized since they'd met that morning. "I was just requesting a copy of that report when you're done."

"You bet," she practically whispered.

Bateman strode across the floor, headed for the door. His

temper had escalated with every step and he aimed his words at the manager. "And I will be turning this over to my lawyer, you hear?"

Johnston wisely chose not to answer. With the swing of a door and a ding of a courtesy bell, Bateman was gone. Everyone breathed a sigh of relief. Guin turned to the old guy. "I'll swing by his place later and remind him of what he agreed to here."

"I'd like that."

She finished the report and gave the store manager his copy. Guin stopped just before the door. She turned toward the manager. "What's Shelby's Mustang Diner?"

April squinted, waited to see where Guin was going with it.

"What?" And then he seemed to realize she was referencing the hat, tossed a look over his shoulder in its direction. "Boy who used to clean up at night left that here. I think it's some titty bar in Vegas."

Both women looked slightly surprised at hearing "titty" from such an old gentleman.

"Blond hair?"

He seemed to think about it. "Don't remember. As I said, he worked at night."

"He still work here?" Guin didn't know how she'd explain this one if the kid walked through the door at that moment. He shook his head and she tried to fill in the blank. "Budget cuts?"

"Not for him. Didn't show up one weekend. He had to go."

"Don't you do background screening on your employees?" April looked around. "I mean you are a security company."

"Budget cuts," he croaked. Old Ted looked like he wished he'd left that one on the ledger.

Guin whipped out her notebook, prepared to write something down.

"Got a name? Last known address?" She smiled kindly when he hesitated. "You know, just in case?"

"Don't recall the name off the top." He shrugged. "He's probably in Vegas."

She put her notebook back into her pocket. "Thank you, Mr. Johnston. We'll be in touch."

Guin didn't require a sixth sense to know the old guy was hiding something.

They started out the door, almost bumped into a young man, wearing coveralls and carrying a tool box, who was on his way in. Guin's elbow brushed against him as they passed. Visionary sparks flew. She turned around. "Hey, excuse me," she addressed him.

The young man turned. He had a tattoo on his neck but she didn't recognize it as a gang tag.

"Yes, officers?" Hispanic accent, white skin.

"Sorry. I thought you were someone else."

He stared at her for several seconds, finally said impertinently, "You thought wrong." He went inside and set his tool box on the countertop.

April could barely wait to get into the car to ask her.

"What just happened there?"

"He's in on it," Guin answered, unsure of how she would explain it. "Gut feeling."

April's eyes went impossibly wide. "Same gut feeling tell you to ask about the hat?"

"Something like that."

April grew very quiet. She started the car, but didn't pull away from the parking lot.

"Christ, please, please tell me you're not one of those cops who has to have all the glory. Keeps everything to herself."

Guin laughed at what she thought was a joke, but the laughter died quickly when she saw the fury burning behind her partner's eyes. She quickly moved to extinguish it. "Oh, hell no. Hell, hell no."

"Look, I'm in no mood to play Watson to your goddamn Sherlock Holmes."

"No way. Listen to me…" Guin scrambled, felt her heart quicken. She'd managed to thoroughly piss off her partner. "Look—I saw that other kid coming in, and vaguely recalled having seen him with another thug wearing that same hat. A blond kid."

"Really?" April said in an uncharacteristically flat voice. Clearly she wasn't buying it. "You remembered a hat."

"Okay, April—this isn't exactly the way I wanted to tell you this, but I have this sort of...gift." Gift? Talent?...Curse? She felt reckless with her impromptu but necessary explanation. "I see certain things that spark these visions of sorts."

"Visions? Like memories?"

Guin watched her. April's interest was piqued, but so had a clear underlying feeling in Guin that she didn't really want to hear anything that might not bode well with her beliefs. Or worse, hear that her partner was cracking up. She'd probably already heard rumors about Guin's possible instability after having her old partner die in her arms. It was in April's eyes, radiated from her like beams of sunlight.

"Like a flashback or something?" asked April.

"Sort of." Guin rolled her eyes. This was tricky, not something that could be explained so quickly or on demand. "But these are very, very concise."

"Oh, like photographic memory, right?" More confirmation that April was guiding the conversation toward something of a saner nature. And she was visibly holding her breath. None of this was promising.

"Yeah, like...that. I guess." And like that Guin indeed saw her partner expel a huge breath. She did too, hadn't even realized she'd been holding one. Obviously this was a secret not to be shared right now. Timing was everything. After all, it would be a challenge to accept for even the most open-minded individual. Guin nodded. "Yeah. You got it."

"Good, okay. I was like..." April rolled her eyes, then smiled a big, relieved smile, and shook her head. "Never mind."

Guin proceeded to capitalize on her lie since it was out there. "I saw the hat, saw the kid, and made a connection. I wanted to talk to the tattooed boy to see how he'd react. See if he got nervous talking to cops."

April's smile faded, her posture softened and she blew a little section of hair away from her eyes. "Guin, I'm sorry."

"It's okay. Don't be." Guin felt guilty as hell accepting an apology when the woman had truly done nothing wrong. Apologizing for utilizing her own gut instinct? If you can't honor that, what's left to honor?

April turned the steering wheel sharply, guided the cruiser out of the lot. They rode toward the station quietly. The mood was a little serious for Guin.

April said after a few minutes. "Do me a favor and we won't speak of it again."

"Sure, what?" Guin looked her way.

April hesitated, shot her a little glimpse, and quietly stated her request. "Just don't fuck me over."

Guin wondered if it was possible she'd met someone as impossibly untrusting as she was. "I won't."

The sushi lunch was a repeat of the dinner they'd shared nights earlier. April had raved about it and Guin was still trying to secure her place back on her partner's good side. It had been a weird morning. As they speared brown rice rolls with chopsticks in a corner booth of the tiny café, the silence gave Guin a chance to think.

Clearly, her "gift" was evolving from a near handicap to something else. For so many years she'd shunned her ability, wished she could be like everybody else, refused to try to understand it. Granny June hated it when Guin referred to it as her cross to bear or her curse. But today it sure felt like it.

She weighed the pros and cons of the curse/gift and the possible outcomes of trying to explain it to April. On the downside, it was going to be hard as hell to explain—April would either get a kick out of it as Terence had, or she would want to get as far away from Guin as possible. With career damaging consequences.

Another downside: having all the answers in advance took the hunt out of the game. Game certainly seemed like the wrong word. Back to the point, April was the one who aspired to be a great detective; to hone her craft, to observe subtleties and tweak clues out of the best camouflage. Not like Guin who only ever wanted to be a street cop. She wondered if April would resent doing hard work versus Guin's easy-out approach.

On another downside, not telling April was deceptive.

Trust was everything to partners. Perhaps if she'd not been so concerned with revealing her psychic self to Cheryl, she would have been able to save her.

It was always there, always on her mind that she could feel things others could not. She considered her mental tally: three downsides, zero upsides. Throw in April's earlier comment about psychic hocus-pocus and she could safely round out a grand total of four.

Splendid.

Guin's internal prattling had her head ripe with a headache. She took a sip of water and slammed the bottle onto the table with more force than she'd intended. Embarrassed, she looked at her partner. April smiled.

"I hope you're still planning to bring that muscle to help me move this week."

Guin chuckled. "I told you I would, didn't I?"

April's smile vanished and her eyes grew distant. It didn't take special powers to know that she was thinking about their words in the car. Guin reached across the table, patted her hand. "Forget about it."

Guin thought about the boy at the alarm company. She needed to make the leap between them, without "magic"— totally on the up and up. Maybe she could use the vision as her guide. Maybe it would inspire her to keep at it until they had the answers they needed. Meanwhile, she had an already nervous partner to deal with.

Guin started shooting in the dark. "Wish I knew where I'd seen that kid before."

"We could check his priors. The tat should be easy to pin down," April said between bites. "See if he hits in CODIS."

"Sure." Guin tried to broach another avenue without insulting her partner. It felt like she was pushing it. "Do you suppose a guy that size could carry all that stuff?"

"Doubtful." April chuckled. Clearly they both recalled the man's delicate frame. It had crossed Guin's mind that he'd adopted his bad-ass behavior to compensate for his lack of height and muscle. Typical. April sipped her tea, dabbed her lips. "Want me to check known associates?"

Guin took a deep breath, went for it. "We could find out where he hangs out…"

"Like that Mustang Diner, or whatever." April was becoming more enthused with her mystery solving. Guin was feeling guilty as hell for spoon-feeding it to her.

"Yeah, maybe pass around a picture."

"If we find something I'll fax it to them this afternoon." She blotted her lips again, balled up her napkin. "You don't suppose it's that old guy, do you? The little sweet alarm company manager?"

Couldn't be. Wrong path. Guin wrinkled her forehead.

"Or maybe not." April brushed the crumbs off her hands and stood. "You ready, Sherlock?"

The name inspired guilt within her. "Don't call me that."

They tossed their trash into the garbage. "Really? Because the name Watson is sort of growing on me."

Guin's lips twitched into a crooked smile. "No."

"Who do you want me to be?" April asked the question in a playful, sexy voice. She made a show of sweeping the door open for Guin, stood back and let her pass.

"Oh, God…" In as many times in a day, Guin felt like a hormonal fifteen-year-old boy.

April brightened. "How about Nancy Drew?"

Guin popped the locks on the cruiser.

"Nancy Drew is a damn-site hotter than Watson."

April smiled; her eyes twinkled in the afternoon sun. "No shit, Sherlock?"

Guin rolled her eyes, laughed. "Get in, Nancy."

CHAPTER SEVENTEEN

The front door of April's old apartment was already propped open when Guin arrived. Peering through a tiny space in her armload of boxes, she double-checked the number beside the door anyway, 469. Right place. Guin glanced down either side of the somewhat dingy hallway. A diaper-clad kid too tiny to be in the hallway by himself stood watching her. The leftover smell of grease and spicy food hung thickly in the air. The immediate assessment had her happy April was leaving the place.

Sergeant Paul Winters almost ran smack into her, causing her topmost boxes to nearly topple off the stack. Guin rebalanced, shot him a look.

"Look out, Marcus," he kidded her. He maneuvered a dolly over the apartment threshold, guiding a chest of drawers into the hallway. Guin was struck with a pang of jealousy that he was already sweaty, looked hard-worked, and clearly had been he-manning the heavy stuff around with ease. He nodded at her, kept teasing. "What? You sleep in today?"

Guin shrugged it off. Jealousy was ridiculous. Besides, Winters was like a brother to her; one of her top three choices for partner before April came along.

"Uh, she called this morning in a panic." Guin set the boxes down just inside 469. "I've been all over the place hunting these things down."

"Good man," he genuinely congratulated her. He always said stuff like that to her, and he really aimed to treat her just like one of the guys. He went on. "How are you anyway, Marcus? You adjusting well? Feeling good and all that?"

He took a quick break, leaned against the chest of drawers in the hallway, actually waited for her answer.

Guin nodded. "It's been hard. But I'm doing a lot better now."

"Good." He nodded solemnly. "Partners run deep. You don't get over that stuff easy."

"Yeah, we know that firsthand," said a new voice.

The voice belonged to Clive Burnette. He appeared in the doorway, feigned emotional pain and clapped his former partner on the arm. "I just can't quit you, man."

"Oh geez," Winters muttered, shaking his head.

Guin rolled her eyes, chuckled at the *Brokeback Mountain* reference. "Will you two lovebirds get out of my way so we can get this kid packed up and outta here?"

Winters worked the dolly, put his back into it. He hoisted the chest of drawers slightly back and began a slow trundle down the narrow hallway. Burnette leapt after him, playfully. "Paul, don't go. You complete me!"

"I complete you, eh?" he could be heard saying. "You're the one who went all detective on me, bastard."

Guin shook her head at the pair. She entered the small apartment and spotted a number of clearly marked boxes. Several of them said "kitchen" in bold Sharpie and Guin pursed her lips as she considered them. April might actually spend time in the kitchen. What a nice switch that would be from her steady diet of takeout. Guin considered that if forced to pack her own kitchen, a single box would do the trick, and more than likely it would be full of leftover condiments and whatever stray beer she had in her fridge. Not that she was planning on April doing a lot of cooking for her. Not that she was planning anything at all.

"Oh good, more boxes!" April's chirpy sound jarred her from her daydream. She hefted another box on top of the growing stack of kitchen boxes and came toward Guin. "Howdy, partner."

"Hey, looking good around here." Guin gave the place a once-over. "We'll have you out of here in no time, huh?"

"And not a moment too soon, for sure." April stood on tiptoes to check the top of the refrigerator. She then made a second check of the cabinets, opening each one and letting the door fall gently shut.

Guin took the opportunity to study her partner. It was the first time she'd seen her out of uniform, not counting their track-suit happy hour. And excluding her starring appearance in a rather high-definition vision, of course. April wore tattered, low-rise, tight-fitting jeans and a paper-thin T-shirt that hugged her just as nicely. Her long hair dangled down her back, messily, Megan Fox-ish. Guin figured the whole package was as good a reward for bumbling Winters and Burnette as money in the bank. Guin bit her lip to fight her smile. She bet April played hell on some men's fragile self-esteem.

"Lucky me," Guin muttered unconsciously. But when her partner shot her an odd look, she hurriedly amended the dangling statement. "Lucky that I found these boxes. They were just tossing them out back of Express Printing."

"Brilliant." April's smile lit up the dim place. "They're perfect for the rest of my dishes. Can you pack them?"

Guin eyed the last full cabinet and what looked like expensive wedding china. She felt nervous. "I don't know how to pack stuff like that."

"Pack them like you would your own dishes," April answered nonchalantly, and shrugged. "You have plates, right?"

"Paper."

April mouthed "yikes" and then added, "We need to get

you eating off something other than Styrofoam. Leave that to me."

Guin's smile twitched helplessly.

"Meanwhile, there's another dolly in the bedroom. You can start loading some of those boxes if it makes you more comfortable. Nothing breakable. Just my under-things and such."

The very mention of such intimate garments had Guin melting inside. She left the room before April could see the impact of her words. She went to the bedroom, located the rented dolly and started stacking boxes on it. They were lightweight enough, probably chock-full of panties, she fantasized. And there were plenty of them—enough for three, possibly four trips, Guin figured. She grabbed one more box and started to give it a little toss onto the top of the stack. But it was full of far more than clothes. Guin held it to her chest and listened to its story.

April had been arguing with an attractive, very thin young woman. Clearly upset, April followed the blond-streaked waif to the door.

"Lauren, wait." April gently touched her arm.

"Don't tell me what I can or cannot do!" The woman jerked her arm away. "I don't need your permission to go out with my friends."

"You were out all night!" April said. "All you had to do was call me if you couldn't come home. I would have gone anywhere to pick you up."

The woman Guin now knew as Lauren only stared at April. It begged the obvious question. April clenched her eyes shut, tipped her chin slightly, remained composed. "Are you sleeping with her?"

"You and I are finished," Lauren stated succinctly.

The look on April's face was heartbreaking. Before the door could slam, Guin threw the box on the top stack to break contact and end the second-hand torture. No surprise, she figured. Everyone has a story, why should April be immune? Still, the scene played out in the back of Guin's mind for a better part of the morning.

They'd packed the U-Haul full by early afternoon. Knowing the bulk of the work was done, April volunteered to thank them by picking up lunch on the way to her new place. Burnette and Winters said they'd go on ahead and April handed the keys over to Guin.

"Wow, I'm in charge of breaking in the place, huh?" she teased her partner. "Ceremony, formal ribbon cutting, the whole works?"

"Go for it." April patted Guin's arm, smiled. "Of course you'll have to unpack everything to find the scissors. But feel free, by all means."

Guin looked at Burnette and Winters, put on her official voice. "Attention movers. The ribbon-cutting ceremony has been indefinitely suspended."

"Well, it was worth a try," April said.

Two hours later, protected by a fortress of boxes, the four dined cross-legged on April's "new" living room floor. The spacious one-bedroom was a considerable upgrade, but that didn't much matter to Guin. The neighborhood alone was such an improvement from April's last place, she could literally feel herself breathing a sigh of relief. One less thing to worry about. Not that she worried, of course.

As they ate sub sandwiches, Winters and Burnette, obviously missing their former partnership, queried each other about who worked harder these days. April and Guin were an attentive audience, quietly casting little glances in each other's direction, an action that didn't go unnoticed by the entertainers. Even Winters, with his cavalier attitude and ill-concealed desire to at least win a drinks date with April, seemed to know the score. He'd lost before he'd even begun to actively campaign for her affections. The women's interest in each other, on whatever level, was obvious to the room.

When the silences got longer and the looks more frequent, Guin clapped her hands together, breaking the trance and indicating that much work was yet to be done. She swiped Burnette's barely empty plate out of his meaty clutches, inspiring a round of heys from the men. They finished their warming beers and stood and stretched.

"Yeah, I suppose that truck isn't going to unload itself." Burnette scruffed his hands through his hair. He headed for the door, followed by his counterpart.

Guin began to buzz around the room, collecting food wrappers and discarding bottles.

"Whoa, okay, hon." April laughed. "What's your hurry? You got hot plans later on?"

"No," Guin answered too quickly. She stopped, recouped her normal careless-looking saunter and forced her voice lower. "Well, maybe I do."

April came dangerously near her, countered with her own best low-sexy voice. "Then I guess I better put a wiggle in it, hmm?"

Guin froze, blinked, wondered if they were still in the joke. She watched April utilize a very deliberate, girly wiggle as she walked across the room. Guin's mouth was slightly gaping, and her cheeks burned when she saw that Burnette had reentered the apartment just in time to watch her watching April.

"What?" Guin asked him impatiently. "The show's over, big boy."

He promptly cleared out again.

April returned to the living room with a plastic bag. Guin quietly deposited the trash she'd gathered up and twisted it shut.

"I'll just...run this out to the Dumpster next trip."

"Don't bother yet," April told her. She smiled, seemed herself again. "Stay here and help me."

So much for escape. Guin nodded, looked around. "Where should I start?"

"Grab a box and rip it open. There's a box cutter over there." She waved toward the tiny foyer table. "Tear it all open. I've got no secrets."

Guin retrieved the cutter, recalling quite clearly the vision she'd seen at the last apartment. Nothing to hide, huh? But then again, April was a big girl, and judging from her nice curves, mink hair and eyes that twinkled like she knew something no one else did, Guin would be stupid to suppose she hadn't had her share of relationships.

She sliced open the first box, waited a moment, got an ethereal all-clear and tore into the next one, relieved that nothing was talking to her now.

"Guin, in case I haven't mentioned it, thanks for helping me do this."

"You have mentioned it." Guin nodded, smiled, and tore open another box. "About twenty-two times so far today."

April turned serious. "Make that twenty-three. I really do appreciate it. I know you have other places you could be."

Guin flicked the box cutter closed, noticed April staring at her, eyes twinkling. She was bewitching.

"I'm happy to do it, April."

And truthfully at the moment, there was no place she'd rather be.

CHAPTER EIGHTEEN

The truck was empty and only a few boxes remained in the street. The guys hustled them inside the building, all but throwing them into the apartment. Guin figured they'd seen more than their fair share of girly things and would beeline off to happy hour as soon as possible for testosterone restoration. She hung back, looked over the row of boxes she'd managed to sort out and carry inside by herself. These were marked "linens" and "towels."

Normally Guin resisted making contact with such things. She was fanatical to the point of avoiding hotels whenever possible for fear of whatever secrets the bedding held—in fact damn well OCD about it. In particular, pillows gave a whole new meaning to the phrase pillow talk. They held stories just as sure as if the sleeper had drained out their every horror or happiness via the ear canal. For these reasons, she'd spent many a night away from home, cramped into cheap vinyl upholstered hotel chairs. Talk about your hang-ups. She'd considered investing in a blow-up mattress for the road.

That aside, she relied upon contact with those same types of personal things to speak to her now. She'd been accidentally privy to the breakup of April and Lauren from the day's earlier vision, and now Guin was fascinated by whatever other secrets her partner held. She longed to know everything she could get her visions on.

"Marcus." Burnette had returned to the truck. He grabbed a duffel bag full of towels and tossed them at her. "Think fast, kid."

In an automatic defensive motion, Guin grabbed the bag, clutched it to her chest. She was not disappointed. The visions were growing clearer. This time April was in the bathroom, shower running. Steam billowed through the tiny room, clearing to reveal a tanned, toned body behind milky glass. Guin took advantage of her unusual vantage point to study her slender legs, hint of musculature in her calves as she moved, her taut waist, perky breasts...

Guin gasped, ached with desire.

April raised her face to the shower stream. Water parted her mane of dark, long hair, and it was then that Guin could see she was crying. She appeared vulnerable, sad, like nothing she'd ever seen from her before. It was a world apart from the woman's usual cheerful self.

The water stopped, and April thrust a hand out from the shower curtain, grabbed a towel and emerged wrapped in its whiteness. She leaned against the bathroom wall, tears still streaming. Yes, it had been a bad, bad breakup.

"Guin? Are you all right?"

April's voice in real-time startled Guin from her vision. She blinked hard, nodded.

"Yeah, just starting to get a little worn out, that's all." She was suddenly concerned that she'd implied moving April's stuff was too exhausting, and quickly amended the statement. "But I'm getting my second wind, no worries."

April smiled and sympathetically nodded. Burnette was also there, but his expression was one of near-concern. Guin had been getting that from him a lot lately. She wondered what was going on. She made a mental note that they should talk. Or not.

"Let me thank you again, all of you," April told them for the millionth time. "Honestly, this has been so great."

She stood there beaming, positive energy practically shooting out of every pore. It was like daytime to the darkness of the inconsolable woman in her visions. Guin wondered how she managed it.

"Not a problem," she finally told her. "Let's get the last of this into your place."

Winters cleared his throat. "You need me to follow you to get this truck back to the shop on time?"

"No, that's fine," Guin heard herself saying. And then to top it off, "I'll do it."

"Okay then." Burnette shoved his glasses onto his nose. "Well, that about wraps it up. If you ladies got it from here, me and Paul are going to take off and get a beer."

"Hon, thanks so much, again. Both of you." April went for a hug, saw the wide trails of sweat down the fronts of the men's shirts. Their mutually disgusting appearances occurred to them all at the same time and they laughed, settled on a simple wave goodbye. "I'll see you at work, then. Have a beer for me."

Guin figured she'd take off after riding back from the trucking company, but April asked her back inside. Biting her lip, wondering about all sorts of implications, she agreed and followed her partner like a sheep. Boxes lined the perimeter of the living room. April spun a slow circle, arms outstretched, a huge smile upon her face.

"Looks like I have my work cut out for me."

Guin was still obsessing over the heart-wrenching visions. "How do you do it?" she asked absently, studying her partner in the center of the floor.

"Do what?"

Guin suddenly felt self-conscious. "Always have a smile. How do you do that?"

"Do I?" She took a step closer.

"Yeah, always." Guin forced a laugh. "I mean, you probably sleep that way."

April's expression turned and her eyelashes batted sexily. She playfully arched an eyebrow, took another step closer. "Well, there's only one way for you to find that out."

Her unabashed flirty behavior caused Guin to clench up inside. Her throat felt tight, her chest warm. Other parts...also warm.

"Wow, okay," she half-whispered.

"What?" Another step. "Am I embarrassing you?"

"No. Well, maybe. I guess you are sort of."

"Yeah?" April was close now and refused to unlock gazes. She was obviously pleased to be responsible for Guin's tongue-tied state. "And now?"

"Yeah, even more." Guin's eyes flitted away, she cleared her throat. "Quite a lot, actually."

April tsked, furrowed her brow. They stood almost toe-to-toe.

"Surely not." Her tone went significantly quieter. "Who would've thought that I'd be able to make tough-as-nails-cop Guin Marcus blush, hmm?"

"Who'd have thought?" Guin half-croaked.

A final step closer, and there was room for no more than a breath between them. Guin gulped, felt her eyes water. A faint sweat and musk scent emanated from April. Guin tried like hell not to think about it.

"What's the matter? Aren't you used to aggressive women?" April made a playful round mouth. "Oh, I get it, you like to be the aggressor."

"No, it's, well...it's just that we work together and—"

"And what?"

Guin blinked away every last rule about forbidden work relationships. It's not like she hadn't had one before and she was quickly realizing just how easy it would be to wake up next to April. Her partner's naughty act was playful enough, but she knew April had an emotional and very soft side to her, evidenced by the tears she'd witnessed, and an even softer side to her, evidenced by the erotic glimpse of damp skin she'd seen in the shower. Oh...her visions were dangerous.

Fight or flight?

"Oh boy—look, I should get home. I'm happy to come back tomorrow and help you unpack if you want."

But the time for excuses had expired, a message made clear by April. She lowered her voice, looked her straight in the eye.

"Guin, the only things I want to unpack tonight are my bed linens and towels. Surely you can stay and help me with that." Never compromising her intense gaze, April reached for Guin's hand. "Can't you, hon?"

There was nothing remotely saccharine in her voice; nothing false about her approach. They were just two women, standing there, one asking the other to stay the night. April leaned into her slightly, brought her lips close enough for a ticklish touch, then gently ran her tongue along Guin's upper lip, tasting tiny beads of perspiration that had formed there.

It was Guin's undoing. Hormones shot through her body, she tingled in places that hadn't been properly attended to since she'd been with Cheryl. Her eyes rolled so far back that she thought for sure she'd actually see her visceral brain. It would surely have April's tanned, toned, shower-fresh body imprinted on it... It gave her inspiration. Guin whispered, "Is your hot water turned on?"

"It is," April purred in her ear. "All my utilities are in fine..."— she kissed her—"working..."—kissed her again— "order."

Gone.

"Christ," Guin muttered. She plunged forward, practically attacked April's neck, kissed her way down the curve and landed in the groove of her collarbone. April gasped with desire, ran her hands up and down Guin's body, which was hot and slick with perspiration that had nothing to do with an all-day move. They kissed deeply. They nearly mounted each other on the spot, but Guin stopped. She thought it should be better than that; it should be special. It was the least she could do for April.

Guin unwillingly forced her away slightly, gazed at her, breathless. Too far gone to turn back. She shook her head, as if she were admonishing herself. She clenched her eyes shut for a moment and when she reopened them, she was solidly locked into the most beautiful blue-eyed gaze.

"Come here," Guin quietly ordered her before either could possibly change her mind. They stripped en route to the bathroom, leaving a trail of clothes all the way to a steamy shower.

This time there were no tears, only gentle exploration, and occasional harried, teenage-style groping. They kissed, touched, teased, loved...it was only a small glimpse of things yet to come.

CHAPTER NINETEEN

The smell of coffee wafted through the air and conspired with a breeze through curtainless windows to gently waken Guin. Her eyelids flicked open and she slowly focused on freshly painted, bare walls, a relief in and of itself. She was entangled in sheets that harbored no memories beyond the previous night's marathon-session lovemaking, and in their frenzy, no pillow had managed to make it out of a box. In all, it was a nearly perfect morning.

She sat up slowly, surprised at the aches in her body this day for having satisfied a variety of long-ignored aches in the previous eight hours. Considering what good shape she was in, it made her smile. Indeed, April had given her a workout.

She heard low singing and the shuffling of bare feet on the kitchen floor yards away and hoped she would be greeted by her partner bearing coffee, wearing a smile, and nothing more than a T-shirt. Guin smiled, dropped back into the tangled sheets. She calculated the breeze, the smell of new paint and fresh coffee, the sound of distant traffic and nearby feet, committed it all to memory, hoping she could recall a command performance later when she needed it. Like the tennis ball Granny June had given her.

"Good morning, you." April was suddenly over her, coffee in hand, long T-shirt draped over her athletic, curvy body. It was better than Guin had hoped for. April sat down on the bed, ran her hand along Guin's sheet-covered thigh. "Ready for some breakfast?"

"Yes, I am." Guin sat up enough to take the coffee from her. She waved it beneath her nose, breathed it in, took a tiny sip, but then placed it carefully on the floor beside the bed. She lowered her gaze, made a funny crooked smile. "What did you have in mind? The same thing we had for dinner, I hope?"

Guin easily pulled April on top of her, went to work kissing her neck, having discovered it was one of the woman's most sensitive spots. April lightly moaned, smiled, and then forcibly pulled herself slightly back.

"Our food is going to get cold." But her protest was weak, at best.

Guin appeared to think it over, shrugged. "I can live with that." And she kissed April, guided the thin T-shirt up.

"Aren't you hungry?" April persisted.

"First I'm checking a suspicion. Hang on." Guin kissed her deeply, breaking only to tug the T-shirt over April's head. She tossed it aside, looked down and smiled with much delight. "Commando confirmed."

April playfully swatted her arm, but quickly gave in, all notions of breakfast out the door. Guin gently shifted April onto her back, then began kissing a trail to her toned belly. She'd learned her way around well, knew all the right spots by now, and set out reigniting any smoldering fires left over from the night before.

More than an hour later, breakfast was nearly inedible. Guin ate it anyway.

"I can make something fresh, you know." April skidded about the shiny kitchen floor in sock feet, stopping in front of the stove.

"No way, this is delicious," Guin said between bites of soggy toast. "The best I've ever had, I swear."

April narrowed her gaze, as if she couldn't possibly imagine that could be true. Guin countered with a cross-my-heart motion.

"Now, come over here and sit down, would you?" She patted the only other chair. "You're making me nervous with your... domesticity."

"Am I now?" April plopped down on the folding wooden chair next to her. She leaned onto the tabletop, rested her chin on her palm. The breeze from the kitchen window lightly flapped the opening of the button-down shirt she'd hastily drawn around her, fastened by only a single button. It was a splendid robe in Guin's opinion. April reached over and caressed Guin's shoulder, tipped her head to one side. "You don't like girls who take care of you?"

That gave Guin pause. She chewed on her runny eggs, glanced away as she considered the question. Finally she swallowed, lightly shrugged, softly admitted, "I don't know. I've never really had that sort of thing."

In her imagination, Cheryl would have taken wonderful care of her. This conclusion was drawn solely upon seeing how she'd interacted with her young sons. Very maternal, very loving. Guin hadn't been the lucky recipient of such one-on-one care from her, but thanks to Cheryl, she'd recognize it now. That same warmth and genuine care now shone in April's adoring eyes.

"Well now, that just doesn't make any sense to me," April whispered.

Guin chuckled softly. "Look, I'm not an easy relationship, April."

April lowered her gaze, smiled sweetly. "I don't think there's anything easy about you at all."

The double entendre was not lost on Guin.

"And you're cute," April continued, taking a sip of coffee. "I've always thought so."

"Always? Always meaning for three weeks?" Guin smiled.

But April only shook her head. "I didn't want to sound like some kind of stalker, but I've seen you at those mandatory city functions. You and your old partner were pretty hard to miss."

The sun was quickly shifting on its mission toward the midday sky; it beamed through the bare windows and Guin squinted against it. "Why didn't you ever introduce yourself?"

April looked away, smiled. "Oh, no. I don't do that kind of stuff."

"Too shy?"

"I guess."

"After being with you last night..." Guin set her cup down, leaned forward, whispered, "I can't imagine you being shy about much."

"Well, believe it or not, I don't do well in groups."

"You seem to handle those mucks we work with just fine."

"That's just my game face." April grinned. "I'm much better one-on-one."

"Oh, I can attest to that."

April picked up a piece of the soggy toast and tapped it on the side of her plate. It wilted and she dropped it back down, looked thoughtful. "So, where do we go from here?"

Guin sensed her concern, knew she needed to be careful. She'd never been solely responsible for making anyone happy. There'd always been another woman (or husband, as the case might be) or a child, once even a Doberman pinscher—something or someone requiring a lover's utmost attention. Guin had waited in the wings, willing or not, for her turn.

Things were different with April. Neither of them had anyone—what a novel concept. Now it appeared that they had each other. Foreign territory for Guin. Just thinking about it made her nervous. She needed to test the waters.

"Where do you want it to go?"

April shrugged, but Guin thought she knew better. She clearly didn't want to risk another round of crying in the shower again too soon. Insecurity suddenly emanated from April like fever. Guin clasped her hand. It was a risk worth taking.

"Then we'll go wherever, whenever you're ready." She leaned forward, whispered, "Come here."

They kissed until April broke contact, pulled back a little. Her smile returned, genuine and brighter than ever. "So, I guess you might actually like me a little by now?"

"I guess," Guin teased, pursing her lips. "You're nowhere near as annoying as you were first day on the job."

April found that somewhat amusing. "I was such a pain in the ass?"

Guin pinched her fingers together demonstratively. "Little bit."

"Fair enough." She shrugged, turned more serious. "So, do we need to talk about this? How we'll be at work?"

Another foreign conversation. Nobody had really ever bothered with those details before. Guin mulled it over. Of course they'd have no choice but to keep it on the down-low and hopefully enjoy lots of hot, long lunches...

But unlike with Cheryl, outside work there'd be no need to sneak around; no waiting quiet nights at home with April across town ensconced in the arms of her betrothed. No kids' school programs to schedule around, no worrying that someone would burst into the room unexpectedly. Aside from the fact that interoffice relationships were forbidden, keeping things on the down-low at work would also discourage the inevitable office gossip. The relationship would be what it was; it would be what they made it.

"Let's just take it one day at a time, How's that?"

A bit of worry flickered momentarily in April's eyes, and Guin wondered if she was the type who required commitment words—forever, together...always...

Too much alien territory to cover at once.

"Okay," April said at last.

"Good." Guin sat back in her chair, relieved that the conversation was over. "And we'll...just see where it goes, okay?"

"God, you are cute." April's mood lightened dramatically. Her growing smile was brilliant. "Unbelievably cute."

Guin blushed again. It was the second time she'd blushed in twenty-four hours; probably only the third time in her entire life.

CHAPTER TWENTY

Captain Briggs was back on the job. He sorted through a massive stack of reports bequeathed to him by Lieutenant Sloan during his absence. Her system was admittedly more organized than that of others he'd left in charge before. Still, he'd spent weeks clearing his brainpan and unwinding his tired body. Now with the simple turn of a door key, he was back to square one, tension headache teasing him already. With a welcome back like that, why bother to vacation in the first place?

Top of the stack was the meth lab explosion file. He opened it, rifled through the paperwork. Every I dotted, every T crossed, Burnette's thorough account and picture documentation. The arrest was clean, the evidence solid. Sloan had certainly overseen a thorough investigation and report. Almost.

He skimmed his finger beneath the picture numbers and

noticed they were out of sequence. Spreading the file out before him, he soon amended that assumption and he hoped this would not be a recurring theme running through all of these reports. Three pictures were missing entirely. This was highly unlike Burnette who generally followed protocol to the letter.

Captain Briggs furrowed his brow. It had been a good arrest, but until the trial was over, anything and everything was subject to an appointed legal counsel's scrutiny. Then there was Interdepartmental Affairs always on the prowl looking for lapses in departmental consistency...

A nightmare scenario was quickly unfolding inside his imagination and he could only hope to hell the guy had confessed, making a lengthy case dissection unnecessary. Briggs wouldn't breathe properly until the thing was off his radar. He wondered if the perp had lawyered up already. If so, how good a lawyer? He personally knew some nightmarish court-appointed ones. Now, even tracking down whatever missing pictures would call for a supplemental report for the file and subsequent explanation. In court, every action was suspect. The department was always under fire to deliver the burden of proof.

He sighed, pressed the intercom button. "Sara, I need Burnette in here ASAP."

"Yes sir," came the warbled voice from the box.

Tension headache full on, he rubbed his temples and waited.

Burnette appeared at his office window five minutes later. Briggs was dosing himself with Alka-Seltzer when the detective entered and took a chair in front of his desk.

"Welcome back, Captain." He greeted him warmly, though the room was thick with anxiety. "What can I do for you, sir?"

Briggs shoved the case folder across the desk, tapped the thumbnail photos. "Start by telling me there was a camera glitch and you have the blank stills to show for these missing sequence numbers."

Burnette studied the numbers, didn't answer as quickly as the captain would have liked. He plopped two more tablets into his water glass. Rolled his eyes.

"Wrong answer."

"I didn't give you an answer," Burnette weakly defended.

"You better always play good cop in the interrogation room," Briggs said, disgusted. He leaned back in his chair. "Your avoidance tactics blow."

"Lieutenant Sloan told me which pictures to include." Burnette started out strong, but his voice faltered and he looked down at the file, added, "And which ones to leave out."

Briggs leaned forward on his desk. "For the purpose of?"

"There were some…error images on the stills."

The captain started to rise out of his seat. "Show me."

"I can't." Burnette watched Briggs retake his chair. "Lieutenant Sloan had me delete them from my hard drive. I gave her the only copy of the disk."

"That's against departmental policy."

"Actually, no it's not." Burnette hated correcting his boss. "I was following a direct order given to me by my superior, and at the time, that was Sloan."

Briggs drummed out an indecipherable rhythm on the desk blotter. Finally he nodded, sounding smug with his parting remarks. "That will be all, Detective. I certainly hope this bit of handiwork between you and Lieutenant Sloan doesn't come back to bite us in the judicial ass. Like we need the publicity of a no-brainer meth lab case being tossed out of court."

"Understood, sir."

"Go."

Burnette made as expeditious an exit as possible and Briggs rummaged through his top desk drawer for Tums already aware that it was going to be one of those days.

Guin had made it back home in time to shower and dress for the workday ahead. Her weekend had been spent helping April unpack in a hurry, then taking time to tend to more fun extracurricular activities. April seemed to be nicely filling a major void Guin hadn't even known she had. Even Guin's apprehensions about being with someone, the same someone, around the clock, had somewhat allayed. She'd spent more than forty-eight hours blowing past little emotional barriers with unexpected gusto. She'd figured herself to be edgy, a real runner when it came to heavy stuff. Never had pegged herself as someone to settle down and it was hard to believe she'd adapted to even the temporary co-habitation of just two measly consecutive overnights. She felt absolutely unstoppable.

"Good morning, partner," April playfully greeted her when Guin got in the patrol car. "How was your weekend?"

She didn't miss a beat. "I spent the whole thing moving my girlfriend."

"In more ways than one," April lustfully said. She leaned across the seat and kissed Guin. They parted, smiling. April teased her in a sing-song voice, "Guin has a girlfriend."

Guin pulled away, pretended to shrug it off. "Yeah? You wanna make something of it?"

April's expression turned less giddy. She tipped her head to the side, allowing her long hair to fall over her shoulders. "Yeah, in fact, I do."

Guin considered all the implications. It could get scary. "Good," she whispered at last and kissed her again.

"I want to know everything about you, Guin," April whispered between kisses. "Everything."

Guin felt a small ball form in her throat, tried not to look obvious about her sudden discomfort. Everything? Guin wondered if the woman could handle all her tricks—not just the ones in the sheets. She pulled away slightly, figured she'd regret the words she said next, but was helpless to not go for it. "Okay, I will. In time."

April nodded, reassured. "I've got all sorts of time, love."

Suddenly Guin was thinking about kissing Cheryl for the last time, in this very car, leaned across seats just as she was with April. Guin was struck with the wrongness of the situation, so close in time after her partner's death. She suddenly deepened her kiss, wondered if she were overlapping the women. Alternating images of the women spun through her head at a dizzying pace. Startled, she blinked hard, drew back, tried to clear her mind. April noticed and Guin needed to redirect the subject without being too obvious.

Guin spotted two lidded coffees in the cup holders. Perfect. Her eyes lit up. "Sweet Jesus, is that caffeine?"

"Your favorite kind."

"Just when I didn't think I could like you any better." She took a long swig. Sighed. "I could mainline that stuff after the weekend we had."

"Was it so awful?" April put the car in drive, pretended to pout.

"I cannot tell you how much I enjoyed letting you wear me out."

They grinned at each other.

After several minutes of riding in silence, April asked, "What's on your mind?"

"If I told you a fantasy I had about you arriving at my place looking just like that..." Guin motioned toward her official clothing. "Would you consider...?"

"A little striptease. Is that what you had in mind? Hmm...you like a woman in uniform, no?"

"Perhaps."

She took on a shrink's formal tone. "How long have you been having this fantasy, Officer Marcus?"

Of course she could not say since she'd known Cheryl. She remembered her old partner's rigid rules about uniformed conduct. She remembered Cheryl stripping down to her skivvies to avoid drinking in her blues...

"It's safe to say I've had it for a while, now."

"Very interesting," April said, in her doctoral voice. The crackling radio interrupted their play. "Perhaps we'll explore that in our next session." April hit the button on the radio. "Unit fifty-four, ten-nine please."

The dispatcher repeated the call directing them to a familiar address.

"Roger that," she said, then looked quizzically at Guin. "Again?"

Back at Valley Alarm Company, the women were met by the frantic-appearing owner.

April took control of the situation before the old guy fell down. "Calm down, Mr. Johnston, and tell us what happened."

"Well, this is damned embarrassing, but we got robbed!"

"Let's go inside."

In the office, Mr. Johnston sat on a stool, breathing hard. April whipped out a notebook and pen, readied herself.

"Okay, tell us all about it."

"I normally take the cash to the night drop every evening, but not last night." He scrubbed his wrinkled forehead, clenched his tired eyes shut. "Last night I closed shop and just went to my granddaughter's birthday party. I was running late and figured it wouldn't hurt this once."

He dropped his hand with a slap on his jeans leg. "I'll be damned if my register wasn't cleaned out this morning. It's all gone."

April's eyes flicked upward, she tipped her head slightly. "Mr. Johnston, at the risk of sounding ridiculous, do you have an alarm system?"

"Yes, yes I do! Of course! And I set it every night." He scooted off the stool and across the floor to the button panel. "I put in my code, faithfully. Got a motion detector and the works. I installed my best system—the DR690 Deluxe!"

Realizing that the officers appeared slightly confused at his rambling numbers, he broke it down for them. "Look—if a cat even passes too close to the window at night the sucker goes off! I've had it misfire—but I've never had it fail!"

"Let's settle down, Mr. Johnston, what do you say?" April took his arm and gently led him back to the stool. "Guin, could you get him a glass of water?"

Guin nodded. Johnston motioned behind them to another smaller room that had a kitchenette. She rifled through the cupboards for a cup and filled it with water from the cooler. She was headed back for the main room when a lopsided picture hanging on the wall caught her attention. It was a baby girl— Ted Johnston's granddaughter, she presumed—frolicking in a sprinkler wearing nothing more than a diaper. Guin smiled, nudged it straight with her index finger as she passed by.

In an instant, the contact inspired a vision of the boy in the hat—the same one she'd seen hacking codes in her previous vision. She was stunned. She pulled her finger back and then touched the picture again. Same thing.

Guin set the water on the countertop and snatched the picture off the wall. The vision of the boy in the Shelby Mustang Diner hat was painstakingly clear and growing more dimensional by the moment. Guin unfastened the back of the frame and removed the picture. Behind the baby girl's photo was her suspect in another photo, hat and all. Guin doubted very much that if his picture was hanging on the wall the boy was merely a night janitor.

Guin walked into the next room holding the frame and both pictures. "Is this your son, Mr. Johnston?" She waved the blond thug's picture in front of him. At once, the shop owner's shoulders caved forward. Next his body did as well, and the old man was in a heap on the floor, motionless.

Guin dropped the picture and frame and shouted into her collar mic. "Unit fifty-four! We need a bus at Valley Alarm Company ASAP."

And then she dropped to the floor and administered CPR until medics arrived.

Back at the station, Guin showered and dressed in fresh blues. The old ones had gotten sweaty with her lifesaving efforts and then ultimately were vomit-covered—thankfully not with her own. The old guy had come around, but he didn't look as happy to be alive as he could have.

Guin finished towel-drying her hair and went to meet up with April who was waiting in the lounge. She was hanging up the phone when Guin entered.

"Unbelievable!" April's eyes were wide. "Old Man Johnston just dropped a dime on his own son. Kid has a record. Winters is en route to pick him up right now."

"Poor old guy. Probably knew it was his kid all along."

"Boy, I sure didn't get that from him."

"Sad thing is, now Johnston faces insurance fraud." She shrugged. "Probably he really just didn't want to believe his own kid was ripping him off. Now he'll lose his business. That's a tough reputation to recover from in that line of work."

"How on earth did you know to look for that picture?"

"It was sticking out the back of the frame."

April was still stunned. "And how did you know he was the boy? This is confusing."

"Remember how I said I recognized his associate—the tattoo kid?" Guin was really thinking on her feet today. "He wasn't involved in this particular case, but I saw the picture, acted on a hunch." She shrugged. "Of course, I didn't think my hunch would send him into cardiac arrest."

April shook her head, looked slightly disheartened. "You must have just touched on the old guy's nerves. What an understated approach to getting a confession. Wow, I don't know if I'll ever get that good."

"You will." Guin rushed to comfort her. "Trust me—it was a lucky guess. Soon enough you'll be guessing what these morons are thinking, okay?"

"If you say." April wore a slowly emerging grin. "You're my super-cop hero, Guin Marcus."

"Believe me when I say it was nothing," Guin told her, and she actually meant it.

April scooted considerably closer to her partner, whispered, "How about I arrange a hero's welcome home anyway?"

"Oh yeah?" Guin considered all the benefits that being a supersleuth might offer her after all. She laughed softly thinking about it, made a crooked little smile. "Whose home did you have in mind to welcome me to?"

"Mine," April replied, resolute lust in her eyes. "I'll cook for you. And later we'll make dinner."

CHAPTER TWENTY-ONE

Inside Captain Briggs's office, Lieutenant Sloan was getting her ass chewed out.

"Manipulating and/or omitting evidence?" Briggs tapped the case file for the meth lab explosion. "Now, I don't know how they do it where you come from, but around these parts, we follow protocol. To the letter, Lieutenant Sloan."

"Understood, sir."

"We can't have these scumbags walking the streets because they got off on technicalities—like misnumbered or altogether missing pictures!"

His face was so red, Sloan feared he'd implode on the spot. She dared not say a word, only nodded.

When he finished, she produced the disk and patiently waited for the captain to load it into his computer and open the picture file. He scrolled along, examining the missing shots, and all at once leaned close to his screen for a better look. After several minutes of squinting and general face-making, he ejected the disk and turned back to face Sloan.

"Well?" He waved his hand, prompting an explanation.

"Well, the pictures are...confusing. I didn't find them to be relevant to the case, sir."

He softened noticeably, but didn't look any less perturbed, only funneled his concern in a new direction. "What exactly was I looking at there, Sloan?"

She searched for her words carefully, answered as if by rote recitation. "I believe it's a camera malfunction."

He stared at her for a bit, nodded at last, looking no less stern. "Make sure that's what your supplemental report states when you include it in the file."

"Yes, sir."

"No sense in adding the pictures back in." He stuck the CD in his desk drawer.

She was glad she'd made another copy, and didn't mention it to him. He clearly wanted it out of sight and mind. He gathered some paperwork before him, stacked it tightly together just to be doing something with his hands. Sloan wondered if it had been his intention to fill out those papers and suspend her. Or worse. He looked at her again. "I'd like that report on my desk by this afternoon, clear?"

"Yes, sir." She scooted to the edge of her seat, hopeful for escape. "Anything else, Captain?"

"No—yes. From now on, Lieutenant Sloan, you come to me if you get...this kind of..." He waved his hand again. It was quickly becoming his way of signifying "etcetera." Etcetera in and of itself seemed to newly signify "weird shit."

She saved him from himself. "We don't get it often, sir."

He furrowed his brow. "No, I hope not."

Sloan made her exit.

By now, Briggs was so desperate for a Tums or Alka-Seltzer he was eyeing the chalk in the tray on the board across the office. He shook his head, instead rooted around his desk for an aspirin.

Jace Sloan returned to her own much tinier office, surprised she could even sit down, that much of her ass had been chewed. She practically hurdled her desk in the very narrow quarters just to get to her chair. She sighed, tried to shake it off, did some neck rolls and breathing exercises. A knock at the door interrupted this recovery session.

Detective Burnette appeared in her doorway.

"Can I help you, Detective?"

"Sorry to interrupt you, Lieutenant Sloan, but there's something I need to discuss with a superior officer."

She detected the confidential tone in his voice, wanted to avoid embroiling herself in any more off-the-record conversations for a while.

"Detective, if it's a personal matter, perhaps you'd best take it up with Captain Briggs."

"Actually, Lieutenant, it's about Officer Marcus."

He stepped inside, closed the door behind him though he'd not been invited to do either.

Sloan sighed, shook her head. "If it's about those pictures, I apologize for having misdirected you in the matter."

"No, no it's not the pictures. It's about the day Sergeant Jones was killed. I was there."

That Sloan was intrigued was hard to disguise. "I see. Before you get started, is there anything you're about to tell me that is not in your official report, Detective? Because anything you say here is on the record."

"Yes. No." Burnette paused and Sloan expelled another deep breath. She'd just had a similarly confusing conversation with her boss. She rolled her hand just as Briggs had, indicating that Burnette should get on with it. "The day Sergeant Jones was shot, Sergeant Winters and I were first on the scene. Officer Marcus was understandably frantic. She was blood-covered and trying to revive her partner. She didn't see us right away."

"I'm sure she was in shock."

"Yeah." He paused again. "Anyway, as we made our approach, Officer Marcus ceased lifesaving efforts and stood up. Just like that."

Interesting. "And?"

"And she began…talking with someone."

The office air was thick with mystery. A chill ran up Sloan's spine and she tried to shrug it off. "Talking with whom, Detective?"

"Nobody."

Lieutenant Sloan's expression didn't falter. She appeared to be digesting the information he'd just presented her with. Burnette's face was troubled. He knew what he'd seen—or hadn't seen. Sloan needed to reassure the troops, needed a diversionary tactic.

She slowly grinned, even chuckled. "Clive, you had me going there for a minute."

"But…"

"And believe me, I appreciate the humor today. Lord knows I needed the laugh after the earful I just got from the captain."

But Burnette's expression remained stoic. Sloan could see she wasn't fooling him even a little bit. There was no lightening the mood on this one. Her smile abruptly faded, she rolled her eyes.

"Dammit, Burnette," she muttered at last. "Why'd you bring this to me? You think I like this gray area?"

"Bring it to you?" His eyes went wide. "You think I liked seeing it? Seeing Officer Marcus having a full-blown, eye-to-eye conversation with somebody only she could see? Now, far as I can tell, that can only mean one of two things."

Sloan rubbed her throbbing temples. "I know."

"Either Marcus has gone off the deep end, or worse—she hasn't."

"I know." She said it louder, almost angrily. Her hands fell to the desktop and she stared at the detective before her.

"And when I see pictures like what we had the other day…" His voice trailed off. Clearly he was struggling.

"What are you suggesting, Clive?" Sloan stared him down.

But she knew exactly what he was suggesting, they both did.

"I had a chance to spend some time with Marcus this weekend. We moved Officer Reese into her new place." He appeared thoughtful. "There were times when she just—seemed…off."

"Define off."

"Reflective, quiet...damned weird." He shook his head. "There's definitely something strange going on with her."

"You're telling me you think she's having a breakdown?"

He looked worried. "I'm telling you I'm scared she is."

Sloan studied him as he stood before her desk. She then reminded herself of her mission to reassure the troops. Her smile was forced, but necessary.

"I'll tell you what. I'll keep my eye on Officer Marcus, and you just keep your eye on the ball, you hear?"

He blinked a few times.

"I'm serious, Burnette. Besides, if I take these insinuations to Briggs's office, I'm going to need an ass doughnut to sit on. You and I both know he's famous for shooting the messenger."

"Understood."

Sloan's voice lowered, her eyes went soft with empathy for the detective. "Are you good with this, Clive?"

He arched an eyebrow. "I'm just confused, ma'am."

She nodded. "Understandable. Let me know if you need to talk about it. In the meantime, you keep your head down and keep this to yourself."

"Yes, ma'am."

"And don't ma'am me, Burnette. You make me feel old."

Her effort to lighten the mood was hardly effective. Burnette smiled at her anyway, stood and made his exit.

When the door was shut, Sloan slid open her top drawer and stared at her copy of the picture disk lying right on top. Though she'd only known Guin Marcus for a short time, there was no doubt the woman displayed odd behavior. But compared to what, Sloan didn't know. Maybe the woman was naturally quirky. She wasn't familiar with Marcus at baseline.

Jace Sloan herself had spent time in Afghanistan and was happy to have emerged physically unharmed and relatively mentally unscathed. But that hadn't been the case for everyone in her unit. She'd heard tales of ongoing recovery, even hospitalization, due to severe post traumatic stress. Some folks would never be able to handle even the simplest job again. You don't live through the stuff some of them had and not come out suffering lasting effects.

She would have been more than satisfied with this explanation for what Officer Marcus was going through after witnessing the death of her partner. Weird behavior. Check. Reckless actions. Check. But seeing Marcus's fallen partner's ethereal image in eight megapixel glory?

"No fricking way," she muttered. She fired up the disk, viewed the images again. Sloan shook her head. It was easy to see how Burnette was having trouble coming to terms with it all. She ejected it, dropped it back into the drawer. Just her luck. "Two weeks vacation and I get entangled with the fricking Ghost Whisperer…"

It wasn't nearly as enchanting as the TV show made it look.

CHAPTER TWENTY-TWO

With Ted Johnston in the hospital and his thug-kid in custody, April and Guin buzzed through the remaining paperwork for the alarm company case with their sights set on home. Guin shook her hand out, eyes fuzzy, fingers cramping after the marathon writing session. Amazing how the promise of an after-work reward had her expediting the process.

April smiled, coyly remarked, "Don't wear those fingers out, please."

"Officer Marcus?" Lieutenant Sloan's voice boomed from the doorway. Sloan wasn't a large woman by any stretch, but her voice proclaimed authority.

Guin glanced April's direction, hoped Sloan hadn't overheard her teasing comment and bust them so early into their affair. As it was, if this one lasted, everyone would know about it sooner or later anyway. Guin swallowed hard at the idea of long-term relations. Oh boy.

"Yes, Lieutenant?" Guin answered, her voice high and scratchy like a busted teenage boy.

"See you in my office before you go?"

"Yes, Lieutenant."

Sloan wasn't very good at casual-friendly, but she offered a parting nod in April's direction.

"Jesus, I hope she didn't hear that," Guin whispered.

"You embarrassed about me?" April feigned offense, but quickly smiled. "You better go see what she wants. See you at my place around seven, right?"

"Yeah, sounds good." Guin quickly sat down right next to April, their thighs touching on the couch. She leaned dangerously close, held the paperwork out and pretended to explain things to her for the chance to be that near. She whispered breathily, "This part is done, just needs your signature. And I cannot stop thinking about everything I want to do with you this evening."

April answered by stretching one arm back, giving Guin a glimpse of her sexy lacy bra just beneath her purposely unbuttoned neckline. Guin rolled her eyes back, smiled as April playfully remarked, "To be continued."

Aching with desire, Guin wondered if it was obvious as she strode through the hallway on her way to Sloan's office, her mind fully engaged with the sexual calisthenics the evening would surely bring. She hoped like hell the meeting would be record short. She knocked on Sloan's office door.

"Come in, take a seat."

"How can I help you, Lieutenant?"

"Just a little talk, that's all." Sloan leaned back in her chair, produced as warm a smile as possible. "How are you adjusting, Marcus? You and Officer Reese bonding okay?"

Oh, if only she knew. Guin's thoughts were trained on April's sweet, shapely curves, her supple— "Yeah, I like her all right. She's a good person to have by your side."

And on top. And beneath. Guin smiled, internally laughing at her own jokes.

Lieutenant Sloan was nodding.

"Good." Sloan paused, studied the bright, clear eyes before her. She was pleased to see the officer looking so alert. Perhaps her days of binge drinking and bathroom trysts were behind her. Good. She then remembered the point of the meeting she'd called. "I was reviewing the case for the meth lab explosion. You know the one."

"Yeah, I chased the one guy down the street. Why?"

"Detective Burnette was also on that call."

"Yes, ma'am, he was. What's wrong? Did I leave something out of my report?"

Sloan opened the folder, flipped through the papers. She found the photos that she'd allowed to be submitted for the final report. She shook her head and abandoned the folder, directed her attention toward the keyboard. Sloan then turned the monitor so that Guin could get a look at the pictures she'd brought up on the screen. "I'm just wondering what you think about these."

It was Guin's first time seeing the omitted pictures and she studied them for several long seconds. The shots were of her standing next to what appeared to be her dead partner.

"Is this someone's idea of a joke?" Guin answered at last. Her eyes flitted back to Sloan's. "They've obviously been Photoshopped."

"No Photoshop," Sloan calmly answered, refusing to release her from her gaze.

Guin finally broke away from her stare and looked at the pictures again. She remembered that day, the odd, welcome feeling of warmth around her. Involuntarily she touched her shirt pocket that still contained her partner's stripes. Yes, this much time later. Habit already. She quickly dropped her hand to her lap, looked at Sloan.

"Any other thoughts, Officer?"

Guin shrugged, tried her hand at being nonchalant. "Camera...film malfunction?"

"On a digital camera."

"Especially a digital camera. You know how computers are."

But Guin knew Lieutenant Sloan knew better than that. She'd never felt anything so strongly in her life. What was she going to say now? Yes, she could see her dead partner? Had regular postmortem conversations with her spirit? No way was she going to give this woman anything more than she'd already given Briggs. She'd stunned him with her ability to recall a description of a killer she'd never seen. But she'd had no choice, she told herself. She'd had to help them find Cheryl's killer. It was only right. But now? Tell Lieutenant Sloan anything to further incriminate herself? No way.

Jace Sloan was well versed in the legal improprieties of leading the witness. But Guin wasn't a witness or a suspect. She was a police officer, a woman, a colleague, sitting before her, trying to answer impossible questions. She knew the woman was holding out on her. Sloan offered no bone, got no bite. "Very well."

Guin leaned forward in her seat to indicate that she had someplace to be. She clasped her hands, tried to be casual. "Anything else?"

Jace Sloan wasn't one for sweeping things under a rug. She wondered about her motivation to get to the bottom of this situation. Was it for the good of the department? For Guin's benefit? Or perhaps it was simply her own curiosity…?

"Marcus, I know that you and Sergeant Jones were close."

There was a certain warning in her voice, and Guin felt it all the way to the pit of her stomach. She made eye contact, waited for whatever came next.

"We were pretty close." She gave her that much, no more.

"I know a lot of things." Sloan stared right through her, unblinking.

"Okay."

Each stared at the other as if any moment, somebody would give in, blurt out, break down—anything. Nobody blinked nor budged.

"Fair enough." Sloan clapped her hands together, and the meeting was over. She couldn't harvest the deeply buried secret. But at some point, she realized, it would surface. She promised herself to stand down only for the moment. But it was fascinating, really. "Then have yourself a good evening."

"You too, Lieutenant."

Inside two hours, Guin had gone from having her meddling superior officer on her back to having her sexy partner, undressed, and sitting squarely on her lap. They kissed deeply, quickly escalating their actions right there on the kitchen chair, all thoughts of food be damned.

"Mmm, Guin, give me a minute, hon. I need some air," April said in her heavier than usual Aussie accent.

"Too much?" Guin asked with a smile. "Maybe we should take this into the next room and get you into bed."

"In due time." April snagged her hastily discarded T-shirt with her toe, dragged it toward the chair until she could reach it with her fingertips. She pulled the thin garment over her head, restoring an air of seriousness that had been deferred by their initial harried hello-groping. "First, tell me what happened with Lieutenant Sloan."

"Oh…I'd rather not discuss work. I mean it's not fair. We can't do this—" She dove in and suckled April's breast demonstratively right through her shirt, then drew back, shot her a flirtatious look "—on department time. Why let work talk infringe on our playtime?"

"It's been driving me batty—I have to know before I can properly relax." April was purely no-nonsense.

"I'll properly relax you." Guin sighed, she could see April meant business and they would have to talk about this before they could get to better things. "There was some confusion about some pictures Burnette took at the meth lab and she wanted my input."

"Confusion?"

"No worries, April. Looks like that bonehead Burnette had some problems with his camera and Sloan wanted to know if I knew what could have caused it."

April looked suddenly and thoroughly confused. "Why on earth would you know anything about that? That doesn't make any sense."

Another crossroads. She promised herself she'd tell April about her handicap. Talent. Ability…?

"It sort of does, but it's a little hard to explain."

She seemed frustrated. "I don't like double-talk."

"Then let me be more direct," Guin told her before diving back to April's neck. She pulled April close, but felt her struggle to get loose. She gave up, released her. "What now?"

"Tell me what really happened. Why would she ask you that?"

Guin considered it, approached the subject carefully. "Look, this isn't new business between me and Sloan. We've had a few chats—" She hooked air quotes. "Always throws me off kilter for a little while afterward."

"Chats?" April shook her head. "This is the first I'm hearing of it. How often does this happen?"

"Often enough." She rolled her eyes, her voice dropped to a near-whisper. "And you and me need to keep this a little discreet, if you know what I'm saying."

"What? Did she ask about us?" April drew back to gauge Guin's expression. "How would she know?"

"No, no. She didn't ask. But she's…sort of been in my face about this kind of thing before."

April's weight shifted. Guin could feel her leaving before she even got up.

"This kind of thing? On the job lover stuff?"

Guin blinked, dreaded the conversation. It's not like April wouldn't have found out about her and Cheryl sooner or later, anyway. Her partner was no dummy. She bit the bullet, let it rip. "Cheryl and I were lovers."

April promptly stood up, just as Guin knew she would. She took a step back, gaping, an intensity of astonishment in her eyes that Guin could actually feel.

"Cheryl Jones, your partner? Your married partner?" She sounded completely shocked. "Guin!"

"Relax. It's obviously over," Guin remarked carelessly. But even Cheryl's death didn't seem to alleviate the steep tension in the room. "Come on, April. What can I do about it?"

April folded her arms, shifted her weight to one leg, causing her long, slender leg muscles to sexily reproportion.

"Christ—is this standard practice for you? Fucking your partners?"

"It's not like that and you know it."

"Do I?" April gasped. "How would I know that? I barely know you—and you're so cryptic, it's hard to get a straight goddamn answer out of you about anything."

Guin also stood up, raised her hands defensively to stop the train wreck happening in the tiny kitchen. "Look, I only told you because Sloan mentioned it to me and I don't want her nosing around our business. That's all."

"That's all?" April echoed, hurt in her voice.

"Because I like you, April, and I want to be honest with you."

"So tell me this, if Sloan hadn't confronted you about this affair of yours and...Cheryl's," she practically spat the name, "would you have even bothered telling me? Or would you let me look like a fool to everyone who already knows you were fucking your former partner, too?"

"Nobody else knew."

"Sloan knows. And she's new." April scampered around the kitchen retrieving her clothes. She snagged her jeans off the kitchen floor, shimmied into them. "Who else knows? Burnette? I saw the strange looks you guys were giving each other when we were moving." She was growing more furious by the second. And more hurt, which was the part that killed Guin. "You think this is funny for me? A good joke?"

"No, no I don't think that at all," Guin stammered, trying to gain some sense of control.

"Well, you might have mentioned it before we slept together."

The sudden quiet was overwhelming. The women stared at each other.

The truth that came from Guin's lips sounded hollow. "I didn't plan for us to...be together."

April was angry and hurt. "You planned to be with Cheryl?"

"I didn't plan for that either." Guin stared at the floor.

April shook her head. "You just take whatever twat presents itself to you?"

Guin felt like she'd been slapped. "That's unfair."

"You fucked your old partner and you fucked me." April stormed around the kitchen. She flicked the stove off and removed a pan of water from the burner, effectively calling dinner off.

"Look, I didn't even want a female partner, okay?" Guin was forced to swing into action and actively defend herself. "I asked Briggs to get me a guy—it's not my fault that I got you. I never intended for it to be that way."

"Are you just trying to dig deeper?" April laughed. "You can't control your hormones, so you asked for a partner you wouldn't be tempted to fuck?"

"April…"

"And then you got me?"

"April."

"And then you fucked me." April folded her arms, nodded, smiled even. "Well, fuck you, Guin."

"I don't want to do this."

"You did it already." April took a step back as Guin tried to approach her. "Stop."

"Look, if I didn't want to be with you, I'd have taken off long before now. I would have taken off at the first hint of confrontation, because that's who I am. I'm not proud of it." She paused. "I'm still here."

April seemed to know she was telling the truth. Tears stung her eyes and she blinked them away. "I can't do this right now, Guin. I just need a little time."

Guin stood there a moment longer, finally nodded. "One thing."

She took two steps across the kitchen, approached April while keeping her hands in a raised surrender position. She leaned over and delicately kissed her partner on her newly tear-slicked cheek.

"I like you, April," she said softly. "I really, really do."

Before April could think to breathe, Guin was gone.

CHAPTER TWENTY-THREE

Guin's head pounded her awake and for once it wasn't from coming off a night of hard drinking.

She'd lain awake for the better part of the last five hours, restless with the knowledge that she should be spooning with her beloved. Yes, she believed she did love April. Or at very least she knew she was capable of loving April. Her brain was muddled.

Her hope was that April had somehow slept better than she had. Perhaps with a clearer mind that rest brings, April would naturally conclude that Guin wasn't such a dog. Or perhaps she'd realize Guin was even more of a dog than she'd previously suspected. Who could say? Muddled, muddled...

She rose from bed. Splashed water on her face and dug through the closet on a mission for gym clothes and boxing gear. There was only one constructive way to work out this anxiety.

She hurriedly brushed her teeth and headed for her car thinking about her own stupidity all the way. What possible earthly reason did she have for telling April about Cheryl? She could have stopped after her warning that they needed to be more discreet. The scene played relentlessly in her mind a half-million times, each time getting the same inconclusive results. See what the truth gets you? And just when she was starting to feel really good about something in her life.

Guin sighed, dialed Granny June when she hit Riverside Drive. After six rings, the matriarch's kindly voice sounded brightly down the line. "Hey sugar, what's happening with you this morning?"

"I'm on my way to the gym. You going to be around later?"

"No. As a matter of fact, honey, I'm on my way out to have breakfast with some friends who just got back from an Alaska cruise." Guin heard a sigh and could clearly see her grandmother standing at the window of her country-style kitchen. She wore a sweater over her dress, blue with tiny cornflowers embroidered on it. Her silver hair was wound up, loosely knotted at the nape of her neck.

"I'm sure they'll want to bore me to death with all their pictures. Thankfully the omelets at Vivica's are worth it."

Guin blinked, surprised at the strange energies that were making themselves known to her and refining day by day. "Okay, Granny."

"Are you all right, dear?"

"Yeah. I was just checking on you, that's all." Guin had to smile. "Your hot-rocking social life is definitely trumping mine these days."

"Well, I certainly hope not." Granny laughed. "All right, doll. We'll catch up soon."

"Bye, Granny." Guin pressed the off button, yanked out her earpiece and dropped it next to her phone in the passenger seat.

Parking on Riverside Drive would not be easy this morning. Saturday morning and probably everyone in the neighborhood was at the gym, purging themselves of whatever corporate horrors they'd endured throughout the week. She herself was cleansing emotional ones.

"Not a spot to be found," she muttered to herself. She made a U-turn, started the process over again. A Kia Sportage chock full of kids was just leaving. The gym had a nursery for power mommies. Guin was aware of it but avoided it like the plague. She easily veered her small car into the newly vacated spot and killed the engine. "Now for my next trick…"

Guin poked through the ashtray that was used only for change and plucked out every piece of silver she could find for the parking meter. Mixed in with her pile of discarded pennies were a beer token and a receipt. She snatched up the latter and held it up to the sky for a better look. Fresh-Clean. She'd deposited long forgotten coats there more than a month ago.

All thoughts of perfect parking were abandoned. Guin hastily pulled out of the spot, making way for a happy Jaguar replacement. She headed toward the dry cleaner. No doubt the jacket had been showered with chemicals. Still, there might remain a glimmer of Cheryl. The souvenir stripes had lost their luster, had gradually stopped emitting their ethereal signals that allowed her to visit with Cheryl. She'd figured the timing was good; having met April and all, she'd focused her efforts solely on her earthly relationship. She hadn't received even a weak signal from Cheryl in at least a week. But now she needed her more than ever.

In mismatched pajamas, April felt she was the furthest thing from sexy. With bags under her eyes and an aching back, she was also the furthest thing from well rested, too. Her bare feet shushed against the floor as she wandered into the kitchen of her little apartment to start coffee. She delicately ladled careful spoonfuls of amaretto grind into the filter, then impulsively dumped probably half a cup in. She fired it up and waited for the aroma to bring her around.

And of course Guin was nowhere in sight.

Had she been there, April would have pulled out all the stops, made them a decent breakfast—toasted sourdough egg sandwiches with provolone, a balance of protein and carbs for energy that they would turn around and expend right back in bed.

Welcome coffee smells filled the room and alerted her senses. She grabbed an oversized mug and a tiny carton of half-and-half, and set about to make the world's strongest cup of java. On a quest for further indulgence, she went to retrieve a packet of raw sugar. Her cell phone buzzed across the countertop. She grabbed it up quickly, hoped against hope that it would be Guin. She read the screen, eagerly flipped it open.

"Yes?" April tried her best hand at sounding thoroughly uninterested. She listened to the woman's thoughtfully executed dissertation of apology. Slight rephrasing aside, it was nothing April hadn't heard before. But on this day the words filtered differently through her sad, overwrought brain. She softened, bit her lip, and against her better judgment answered the sweetly stated request. "I didn't sleep well either, love. Please, do come over."

Guin raced through the door and straight to her bedroom, anxious to be reunited with her lost love, Cheryl.

She set a brown paper-wrapped bottle of tequila on the bedside table and promptly got comfortable, stripping down to boxers and a T-shirt. She stared at the doorknob where two jackets in dry cleaner's plastic hung. She stepped closer to the jacket, hesitantly touched the one in front. Nothing.

She raised up the plastic and ran her hand over the smooth sateen. Guin gently pulled it off the wire hanger and buried her nose in its collar. There she detected the faintest scent of Cheryl that even the dry cleaner's powerful chemicals couldn't obliterate. She placed the jacket on her bed.

Guin poured herself a drink and downed it. Liquid courage. With watery eyes, she unzipped the jacket and slipped it on, overlapping the front around her body like a warm blanket. She caught a glimpse of herself in the dresser mirror, studied the jacket.

The scent of Cheryl grew unexpectedly stronger and a

blinding burst of white light reflected off the mirror like a flashbulb. And then she appeared.

"Cheryl," Guin whispered as she gazed upon the most beautiful woman she'd ever had the privilege of loving. "Thank you...thank you for coming."

Guin felt her breath catch in her chest as her feet lifted off the floor. The invisible force took her higher until she was suspended midair over the bed. Just as suddenly, the hold released her, sending her sprawling onto the bed covers. Her arm caught the bottle, sent it crashing onto the Spanish tiled floor.

The bright light infiltrated the room, defeated the sun with its white, fuzzy glow, and warmed her throughout. Cheryl's dark eyes were still locked on hers, but she was helpless to move, paralyzed by the strongest force she'd ever encountered.

The energy in the room all but buzzed as Cheryl took a step closer. Guin desperately wanted to touch her. Then, like an angel lifting its wings, Cheryl spread her arms, igniting a surging energy inside the room. She leapt onto Guin and clutched her tight, held her face to face. Heat radiated from her otherworldly being. Sweat formed on Guin's forehead, back and along the waistband of her boxers. She watched as the jacket slowly zipped itself, clear up practically to her chin. It heated up, creating a mystical sauna. Her head felt light; her body felt as if it were shrinking against the heat. Then there was a voice in her ear.

"You must tell April."

"What?" Guin shook her head, felt helpless. "No, I can't, Cheryl."

Cheryl hovered over her, then her form altered once, twice, became cloudy, different. Suddenly, with the precision of a surgeon's knife, it plunged through Guin's jacket like a loud, torturous waterfall of white light. Guin heard screaming. She realized it was her own voice.

Fighting to get control of her own, seemingly useless limbs, Guin was finally able to yank the zipper down. With the same burst of energy in a reverse action, equally as loud, it left her. And then Cheryl was gone.

Breathing hard, Guin slapped her hands over her chest where the brilliant illumination had been a split second earlier. With no small amount of fear, she wriggled free of the heavy jacket and heaved it off the bed. She eagerly ran her fingers over every inch of her abdomen and chest, checked her arms, eyes wide. She felt exhausted, but otherwise fine. She lifted her sweat-soaked T-shirt to see if she had damaged it in any way. She couldn't imagine how she could possibly have emerged unscathed from the white fire that had plunged into her. Not even a mark. The fire was gone, and she contemplated the possibility that her mind could be as well.

She raised up onto her elbows, examined the spilt booze. It was the only remaining evidence that anything had happened at all. Her eyes flitted nervously about.

"Cheryl?" she whispered to the room. Then a little louder. "Cheryl!"

Nothing.

She sat up, stared over the edge of the bed at the soaking jacket. Then, guarding her footing against the scattered glass, she let shaking legs walk her into the bathroom where she splashed cold water onto her face. She studied herself in the mirror as she blotted her face dry, then dropped the towel and tore the shirt over her head for another check. No, not a single mark.

She didn't know what was happening to her anymore. The way Cheryl's spirit had appeared and then suddenly vanished like a genie being sucked back into the bottle—only the bottle was the jacket.

"What the fuck," she muttered. She clenched her eyes tight, wouldn't even find comfort in the bottle that was now splattered all over the floor. She abandoned the sink and found jeans and a zip-up sweatshirt. Didn't bother with a shirt. She stuck her feet in canvas tennis shoes only for the purpose of getting across the floor, which was peppered with shards of glass.

She'd had her share of ghosts and ghouls for the day. Now she was ready to drink in the company of earthlings. She craved escape from her own home. Anyone with a pulse would be fine company. And if necessary, she'd find someone else's bed to escape to tonight.

CHAPTER TWENTY-FOUR

Guin tried to reach Terence on her way to the bar, but her call was routed straight to voice mail. In previous conversations with him, she'd hinted that her "talent" was expanding to include occasional visions of whomever she was speaking to on the phone. Perhaps he'd considered this and declined to answer for fear of her discovering him in a compromising position with his new lover.

At least somebody was getting some. As for herself, she planned to cure what ailed her by whatever means necessary. On previous conquests, this had sometimes included letting some dame bend her ear with office gossip, insult her palate with pink frou-frou drinks, only to be carted off to some hole in the wall studio apartment harboring more secrets than Area 51.

Guin pushed open the door of the obnoxious bar. It was the

same place she'd come to with Terence, the same place they'd prowled for years, despite multiple name changes on the marquee. The place was living up to its wild reputation tonight, booming music, hot to trot guys and girls, drinks flowing and adrenaline pumping. It was exactly the anonymity that she'd been craving. Guin sidled up to the crowded bar, ordered a drink and pointed the bartender to a side table where she'd be taking shelter for the night.

A tall, voluptuous Italian woman was already giving her the eye. She ignored her. Still, the memory of a different Italian woman she'd once dated left her smiling some. Her name was Allegra, and she'd relied upon her hands as much for talking as she did her full red lips. She'd lapse into her native tongue, leaving Guin bewildered, but there was a different, unmistakable language that they'd had very much in common.

Ultimately, Allegra had accused her of cheating (it's not cheating if you're not committed, Guin had argued), and her frenetic wide-sweeping hand gestures had spelled out in at least two languages exactly what she thought of Guin's tomcatting lifestyle. It was such an exaggerated, furious display that Guin feared she'd get her eye poked out. Nice.

Terence had appreciated the story like no other. When he'd recovered from his fits of laughter, he'd given her sage advice: "In the future, if you're going to piss off an Italian, wear safety glasses."

Guin hurriedly looked away, pretended to study the drink card on the table lest the busty Italian woman mistake her smile to be an invitation for company. She really didn't need people tonight. She really only needed their noisy, anonymous camouflage.

Guin was beginning to actually know the regular bartender. He was the same one Terence had been hitting on weeks earlier. The young guy brought her a shot of Patron tequila and waited on standby with the bottle to refill her shot glass.

"Thanks," she muttered.

"No problem, sweetie." He patted her shoulder gently, a seemingly uncharacteristic move from this muscle-bound beefcake. "You look like you need it."

"You're highly observant."

"I'd leave you the bottle, but this ain't the Wild West."

Guin's lips tipped into a smirky smile. "How about you just keep an eye on my glass."

"Deal." He left and returned moments later, another shot, and a tall glass of water with four cubes.

"Thanks, bud, but I'm not going to want to dilute anything tonight."

"You just keep that water coming." The familiar voice sounded from behind her. Guin rolled her eyes as Lieutenant Jace Sloan slipped into the seat next to her.

"Off duty, Lieutenant Sloan," she warned.

"Hello to you, too, Marcus." She looked at the beefcake bartender, tsked at his low-rise pants and bare chest. "Miller Lite, please."

Beefcake went to retrieve it. Guin downed her fresh shot, set the glass on the table, cringed and dabbed her lips with a cocktail napkin.

"You're starting a little early with the hard stuff, aren't you?" Sloan prodded. She sipped her beer, appeared to thoroughly enjoy it.

"Better late than never." Guin motioned toward the bartender. Feeling a slight buzz, Guin smiled, puffed out her chest. "You don't get to be a power drinker like this without training for it."

Another shot in front of her and Guin started to lift it to her lips. Sloan caught her hand and led it back to the table. "Have you had anything to eat yet, or are you existing purely off your recommended daily allowance of Agave?"

"What are you, a Virgo or something?"

"Ouch, now that's an insult," Sloan joked. Guin stared at her for several second before breaking into a small crooked grin.

The shot glass was well out of reach and Guin couldn't retrieve it without leaning clear across the flimsy table. She could see the entire works crashing down in an embarrassing tequila recovery effort. She looked at her only other option, reluctantly raised up the glass of water. "I'd toast you to that one, but a water toast is bad luck and I don't need anymore of that."

Sloan smiled. "So tell me, Marcus, what brings you out this evening?"

She shrugged. "Needed to get away."

Across the bar, a beautiful actress-type had been trying to establish eye contact with Guin. She finally did and they traded smiles.

Sloan noticed the exchange, absently asked, "What would April say if she saw you flirting like that?"

Guin watched her superior slug back a drink and coolly wait for the answer. Instead she got a question. "What's that supposed to mean?"

"Marcus, don't play me for a fool. I've got eyes and a brain. You've got that coy little attitude and some freak...hormonal condition you can't seem to satisfy. Of course you're doing her."

"No—you've got it wrong, Lieutenant."

"For starters, it's Jace when I'm off duty." She took another drink, added. "Like I'm going to sit here and have a sex-chat with you calling me Lieutenant."

"Sex-chat?" Guin couldn't help but grin. "Is that what we're having?"

"I'm not here to chastise you about whose panties you're getting into these days."

"Panties?" Guin was growing more amused by the moment. She leaned back, got a good look at her to see if they were seriously having this odd-ass conversation.

"You're not the only one who's got issues. Everybody's fucking somebody."

"Are you?"

Sloan tipped her head, blew the bangs out of her face with a hmph. "My partner and I just had a baby. I'm not fucking anybody." She took a sip of beer. "Of course that doesn't mean I'm going to go out trolling around to get some. I mean if your woman's good enough to expel something the size of a nine-pound bowling ball from her va-jay-jay?—you're going to hang around, you know?"

"I don't know much about commitment," Guin admitted. "And I'm in no hurry for bowling balls."

"Seems you fish out of the work pool a lot, is all I'm saying."

Sloan shrugged. "The LAPD has it on the books that they forbid on the job male-female relations. So technically you haven't broken any rules."

"They haven't caught up with that one yet, huh?" Guin tipped her head to the side, considered it.

"They work with you for long and they will catch it, I guarantee it." Sloan gave a look across the room at the actress woman who was still working hard at getting Guin's attention. She narrated her summary: "Oh brother. A pulse with a nice set of walking sticks."

"Can I have my shot, please?" Guin was eyeing the glass on the other side of the table.

"First drink the water. Didn't your mother ever teach you to pace yourself?"

The thought of Gloria teaching her anything whatsoever constructive or healthy was enough to make her throw her head back and laugh.

"I'll take that as a no." Sloan waved at the beefy bartender. "One more beer, two waters, please."

Guin downed the water and was rewarded with an eye-roll and the long-awaited shot. She savored this one, suddenly realizing there might not be many of them in her future on this night. "So, you're married, then?"

"Nope. We're domestic partners." Sloan thanked the bartender, handed over her empty glass and sipped the water first before the beer. Good example. "I'm not into paperwork."

"Me neither."

"But I'm into loyalty," Sloan said, lowering her eyes condescendingly at Guin. "You hear?"

Guin's eyes went big. "I'm not trying to get into your pants."

"As you better never be." Sloan calmly raised her water glass and they clinked shot glass to water in a toast. "So tell me why you're here instead of home with your new Miss Thang."

"Tell me why you're here instead of home with your partner and new baby."

"She's hormonal as hell. Three hours ago I told her I was going to the garage. She thinks I'm building a crib."

Guin didn't know if she was serious or not. Either way, the thought of it made her chuckle. It was hard to believe, but Sloan wasn't so bad after all.

It was Guin's turn to answer the April question. "We fought."

"Over?"

"Cheryl."

Sloan seized her slight opening into the subject. "Now that's plain ridiculous, don't you think? Jealous of a dead woman?"

"It's complicated."

"How so?" Sloan waited but got no answer. She slightly shifted the subject. "Speaking of work stuff—which I don't like to do when I'm not there—that was solid work on that alarm company case."

"Thanks."

"The way you were able to take the little bit of evidence, not a single eyewitness, and still get a full confession out of that shop owner is nothing short of amazing." She stared Guin down, added in a darker voice, "A damn well, highly unlikely miracle."

"Well, we examined the computer for—"

"Bullshit, Marcus," Sloan interrupted her. "I don't like to be lied to, so let me just stop you there. Besides, you can't even turn on a computer. You repel technology."

That was sadly true. Guin only stared at her.

"Now, what's the real truth?" Another shot arrived at the table, summoned by Guin. Sloan intercepted delivery and held it next to her water, waiting for an answer. "So what's the story," she baited. "You psychic?"

Guin blinked several times. A crowded, noisy bar, drinks flowing, a hot nameless actress giving her a come-hither look from across the room, and she was sitting here with her superior having this conversation? Now?

Guin nodded. "Sort...of."

"Now that didn't kill you, did it?" Sloan pushed the shot across the table in her direction. "Here's your reward."

Guin downed it with such alacrity, her eyes watered.

"So if I got this right, nobody understands the poor little psychic girl, so you come here to drink to dull your senses." Sloan leaned forward, grinned. "All six of 'em."

Guin went suddenly serious. "I don't feel sorry for myself."

"You sure about that?"

"How did you know, anyway?"

It was amazing Sloan could even hear Guin's low voice so deeply imbedded was it in the crowd noise. The lieutenant pulled a folded picture out of her jacket pocket, smoothed the crease and slid it across the table.

There she was, with dead Cheryl. Guin folded it closed, reluctantly slid it back.

"Oh, you can keep it," Sloan told her. "Creeps my girlfriend out, anyway."

Guin's expression changed again. "You told your girlfriend?"

"I tell her everything because I trust her," she said in a chastising voice. "You could learn a thing or two about how that works, from what I'm gathering."

"Coming from the woman who's supposed to be building a crib," Guin mumbled.

Sloan grinned, raised her glass high. "Cheers to that."

"Amen," Guin said, and slammed another shot. They set their empty shot and beer glasses on the tabletop. The bartender knew the routine by now, returned with water.

"So, you want to ask me how I do it?" Guin wriggled her eyebrows. "How I see dead people?"

"I don't even care how you do it." Sloan took a long chug of ice water, set the glass aside. "I'm just wondering if there's a way we can get your head on straight off the job so you can be your best person when you're clocked in."

Guin's smirky smile faded. She nodded. "Could take some work."

"I take it April doesn't know about this."

"No."

"Did I scream and run away?" Sloan waited for Guin to shake her head. "She won't either. You've got to give people credit."

"I can't control it—who I see or when. It's like a...trance." It was a strange confessional coming from Guin, but Sloan held back, let her clear the decks. "With Cheryl, sometimes I can see her very clearly, like she's standing right here. We talk, believe it or not. And sometimes when I need her, I can't find her anywhere."

"You know what would be nice?" Sloan reached across the table, patted Guin's hand. "To see somebody alive make you smile as hard as you were in that picture."

Even in her advancing stage of inebriation, Guin realized what had just happened her. She said, simply, "Thank you, Jace."

CHAPTER TWENTY-FIVE

Guin had new appreciation for her former partner these days. Previously, Cheryl would go to the station every morning extra early, trade her car for the squad car, and then come to pick up Guin, like clockwork. Guin was not as early a riser as Cheryl had been, but she supposed having a husband and two small children to look after would probably require routine. Such was not Guin's strong suit.

On this morning, she nervously pulled into the first parking spot in the parking lot of April's apartment building and waited. She hadn't even talked to her partner since they'd had words several nights earlier; didn't know for sure if they were still sticking to their routine of morning pick up or not. She was there strictly on the faith that time had healed...something.

She'd begun to think the worst by the time April emerged

from the front door, two cups of coffee in hand. She dropped into the passenger seat, even smiled like it was just another day. But Guin held her breath not quite trusting the odd tremor in her consciousness.

"Good morning."

"Good morning."

Fair enough. April handed her one of the steaming cups. Guin took it; shot her a little insecure glance.

"I had time to think about it."

Guin was thankful that April was getting right to the point about "it," and quickly, too. She hated the suspense. "I suppose it could be purely coincidental that you happened to sleep with two women who just happened to be your partners."

Guin expelled the breath she'd been holding. "Thank you for seeing it my way."

"Even though we're the only two female partners you've ever had, and you did sleep with both of us."

There was a dangling note of allegation in her statement, but overall, Guin thought April seemed even more confident than she had during the entire time she'd known her.

"Okay..."

April took ownership. "And in fairness, I am the one who came on to you."

"Not that I didn't want you to." Guin felt it was only right to extend a confession on the tail end of April's. They were clearing the air. It felt good. "And I missed you a lot this weekend, April. A lot."

"Really?" April slyly grinned. "How much?"

Guin rolled her eyes, chuckled softly. "Enough to go to Masquerade and come home totally alone."

"Masquerade?" April tipped her head, quizzically. "Isn't it Faces now?"

"Who cares, it's a meat market." Guin shook her head. "I thought being with someone would be better than being alone. But that wasn't true." She looked April straight in the eyes, spoke with purpose. "There's nothing like being with you."

"Oh baby..." April reached across, stroked a curl out of Guin's eyes. "I can't tell you how glad I am to hear that."

Guin smiled. "And I actually had an unexpected companion that night."

April nudged her hand away, prepared to be hurt. "Oh, really?"

"It was Sloan."

"Lieutenant Sloan?" April's eyes widened dramatically. She practically gulped out loud. "Our Lieutenant Sloan?"

"The one and only." Guin nodded. "I guess she lives nearby." She started the car, backed out of the parking space. "Doesn't surprise me. I've seen her there before."

"Oh, wow..."

"And not to make you nervous, but she knows," Guin stated quite simply.

"About us?" April wasn't nearly as calm about it. "You told her about us?"

"No, she actually told me. She knew about Cheryl, too. Woman doesn't miss a trick."

"How's that possible?"

Guin gave a little push. "Maybe she's psychic."

"Get serious." April's quick discounting of the notion set Guin's senses on high alert. "Not cool. Not cool at all. I need this job, Guin. I love this job."

"Relax. She won't say anything."

April's eyes flashed with intrigue. "You have some dirt on her?"

"Seriously? Blackmail a superior officer?" Guin shot her a look before pulling onto the main road. "No thanks. Besides, I don't need to have any dirt on her. I trust her."

"You trust her?"

"Yeah." Guin shrugged. "I have a good feeling about her."

April didn't look reassured in the least. She rubbed the lines in her forehead, gazed out the window. "And I suppose you're psychic now."

"Would that be...all that bad?"

"Get serious," April remarked for the second time.

Guin kept glancing her way, but April clearly was preoccupied with the notion that Sloan would rat them out. Guin, meanwhile, was preoccupied with the notion that April thought psychics were a fraud.

Guin finally broke the silence. "Listen, don't worry, okay?" She reached across the seat and gave April's hand a quick squeeze. "It's okay. Trust me."

April's posture relaxed. She nodded, smiled at last.

"So, since we're sort of normal again, you want to have dinner tonight?" Guin gave her partner her undivided attention while they were at the stoplight. "We can talk. I mean really talk."

"I'd like that."

"Yeah?"

"Guin?"

"Yeah, baby?"

"We're not going to get to tonight if we don't get to work today."

Guin regarded her partner's sly smile, suddenly noticed the honking behind her despite the fact that they were in a patrol car. God only knew how long ago the light had changed.

Guin snatched up the loudspeaker microphone and made a bold, ridiculous announcement. "Quit honking, or I'll issue every last one of you a noise citation, I swear to God."

"Guin!" April's eyebrows practically hit her hairline. When she saw Guin's funny smile, she threw her head back and laughed. "You are really going to get us into trouble!"

Her laughter was a beautiful sound. As they pulled away from the stoplight, April couldn't hold back any longer. She unbuckled her seat belt and scooted close to Guin. She kissed her neck, unbuttoned the top button of her uniform, and suddenly each woman knew she'd be no good until she'd gotten the other out of her system.

They barely made it to Guin's pool house, crashing into the tiny flowery hedge, fumbling with keys and tripping over the low threshold. They were naked before they even made it to the bedroom; a trail of clothing in their wake gave a clear timeline of their escalating passion.

"You know," Guin said between frantic kisses. "Sometimes make-up sex just cannot wait."

"We shouldn't waste any time," April wholeheartedly agreed. Guin pressed her body against her partner's warm, smooth skin, reveled in the intimacy.

"We should have gone to your place," she whispered. "We'd be a lot closer to the station."

"Yeah, we could be late."

"I hope we don't miss any calls," Guin continued, but her concern didn't slow her frenzy any. Her hand wasted no time finding April's vee.

"Yeah, we could get into a lot of trouble."

Guin traced April's already soaking lips with her fingertips. She teased her with a flicking motion that she'd already learned April liked.

"I hope we don't—"

"Guin," April said, desperate and breathless. "Shut the fuck up."

With that, Guin plunged herself deep into April, kissed her, bypassed foreplay and fucked her with the zeal of a lover who'd been gone too long, despite the fact that it was merely a weekend. April's moan emerged like a deep growl, nothing Guin had ever heard out of her before.

Guin shifted her arm, swung April on top of her for better access. She went deeper, harder, pulling out between moans, causing April to writhe with delight and scream for more. Guin smiled, wondered what her fancy-pants neighbors would think of the early morning ruckus. She hoped every last one of them was jealous.

Another slick plunge sent April over the top. She shuddered as her body exploded and at last she collapsed on top of Guin.

"Oh, hon…" she whispered coarsely. "Oh…holy shit."

Guin edged onto her side, kissed a trail over April's breasts and up to her collarbone. She bit the leather corded necklace April was wearing. In a flash of light, she saw April standing before the coffeepot in her kitchen, preparing two cups of coffee. She heard someone humming a Black Eyed Peas song; saw her dump in a creamer and two sugars into each cup. The vision vanished as quickly as it had appeared. Guin smiled, closed her eyes, relished in the feeling of being with April.

April teasingly chastised Guin for ticketing an old guy on the way to the station.

"We can't walk into that place late and empty-handed, now, can we?"

April laughed hard. "Guin, he was a hundred years old!"

"A hundred-year-old dude going fifty in a thirty-five is clearly a danger to society."

In fact she had felt a little guilty for issuing the poor guy a ticket. But that's the price you pay when you miss lineup because of good sex, she consoled herself.

Nobody seemed to notice that the pair was even late. This point wasn't lost on April, who teased, "Aren't you ashamed of yourself now?"

"No way, totally worth it."

After a largely uneventful shift, Guin dropped April off at her apartment.

"I'll be back after my run with Terence," Guin promised between kisses. "I've been blowing him off lately. I owe him."

"Dinner?"

"At very least." Guin wriggled her eyebrows playfully. "I'll drop back by in a couple of hours, how's that?"

April looked thoughtful. "I have a bunch of pictures lying around I need to hang up. Make the place look a little more homey. You know what I mean?"

One woman's homey is another woman's nightmare, Guin mulled. "I guess."

"So, why don't we meet at your place?"

Guin made a funny round mouth. "Oh, an encore. I'd like that."

CHAPTER TWENTY-SIX

Guin's long strides had her ahead of Terence by at least twenty yards as they ran along the Los Angeles Reservoir. But then she stopped, doubled over and waited for him.

Sweaty and breathless, he jogged to catch up. "Hey," he called out as he reached her. "There's plenty of track left to leave my ass in the wind. What gives?"

"Tired," Guin said between uncharacteristic pants. "Need water. Air."

"Thank Christ," he muttered. Terence uncapped his water bottle and handed it over. "Catch me up while you're catching your breath."

She flashed him an inquisitive look. He rolled his eyes, hooked air quotes. "Your lesbian drama." He laughed. "You never finished telling me why you and April spent the weekend apart."

188 Linda Andersson and Sara Marx

Guin took another slug, wiped her lips on her jacket sleeve. "She freaked when I told her Cheryl and I had a thing. But I think we're good again."

"She's good about you trying to get your freak on with Cheryl's ghost?"

Guin's eyes bulged. "I didn't get my freak on with anyone." She shook her head, looked concerned. "And I didn't tell her about my...talent."

Great, he mouthed. Then, "I thought that seemed like a quick recovery. Lesbians never do anything that isn't dramatic or drags out forever."

He waggled his fingers in the air. Guin shot him a look, waggled her jazz hands right back at him. "Nice stereotype. Turn the flame down, Terence."

"I'm just saying."

"Look, April's a great girl. I really like her."

"But you don't trust her."

"I do." But her voice lacked much conviction. Still, she had to admit, "I could really fall for her."

"Then you have to tell her."

She shook her head. "It's not that simple. She doesn't even believe in her own horoscope." Guin chuckled. "And you have to admit, it's tough information to swallow."

He shrugged. "I came around quickly." But he seemed to see something different in Guin's eyes now. He smiled; his voice was full of sympathy. "You're in love, aren't you?"

"I'm not ready to say that yet."

"You don't have to." He took the bottle back from her, tossed back a swig. "Don't worry so much about an occasional argument. Besides, a little make-up sex never hurt anyone."

She wholeheartedly agreed. "Yeah, it was nice."

He shot her a look, playfully smacked her arm. "Already?" His voice raised three octaves. Then it dropped to whisper level, and he looked semi-disgusted. "But not in the patrol car, right?"

"Yeah, in the middle of LA with all its traffic cameras." She lowered her eyes. "No, Terence. We went to my place."

"On the clock?"

Guin ignored him. They started downhill toward the car.

"Holy crap! You could get into so much trouble."

"Dude, how do you think me and Cheryl used to get together?" She clicked the remote locks. "Think about it."

"So you're doing something tonight?"

"Yeah, she's supposed to come over in an hour or so." She glanced at her watch. "But you know, I think I'll go over to help her hang pictures instead. Surprise her."

"Wow, this is getting stranger and stranger by the moment." He plopped into the passenger's seat, looked dazed. "You are voluntarily handling someone's personal effects, all visionary notions aside. It must be love."

With a dozen long stem roses lying on the seat beside her, Guin waited at the light at South Coyote Canyon. She held her phone up, willed it to have better reception, but tower bars were fleeting in these parts. When her screen lit up green, she hurriedly called April's number.

"Hey, baby." April's spirited voice sounded down the line warming her on the spot. Guin smiled. "How was your run?"

"Ended a little earlier than I'd planned."

"You want me to come over sooner?"

"Actually, I had a different idea in mind." She glanced at the flowers, but was suddenly assaulted by a vision of April fussing over a pot on the stove. She saw April chatting as she chopped peppers and onions, scooted them off the cutting board into the kettle. Guin didn't know if it was a real-time or recycled image. "Are you cooking?"

"I am," she confirmed. "I was throwing something together for our lunch tomorrow. It's always better the next day."

Guin saw her again. Her eyes narrowed as she studied the pot. "Is it...chili?"

"It is," April's voice was a mixture of amusement and puzzlement. "How did you guess that?"

Guin smiled. Maybe she'd tell her tonight. But not this moment. "Just lucky."

"Incredible."

Guin's smile abruptly faded as the vision came into view again. This time she saw arms wrapping around her girlfriend's waist. Her vision panned a little further out. It was Lauren, and April was nuzzling her face against her chest. There was a telephone to April's ear. At the same time her lips moved, and Guin heard, "Hon, are you still there?"

The light had turned green long ago and it was the honking of several horns that drew her out of the miserable vision. She made a U-turn right in front of everyone, nearly causing chaos in her wake. Her voice was edgy, hurt. "I'm here. Tell Lauren I said hi."

She flipped the phone shut, tossed it into the seat beside her.

April stood in the kitchen; her hand froze from its stirring motion. She set the phone down, utterly puzzled.

"Was that your partner?" Lauren casually asked.

"It was." April unwound herself from the woman's arms, smiled, and said, "I have to go out, hon. Go ahead and eat without me."

Guin continued down Barham, going faster than the speed limit, but it was really the last thing on her mind. She continued to ignore the phone buzzing on the seat beside her. She reached across the seat, grabbed the flowers and threw them out the window, paper and all.

April zipped up the long driveway that led to Guin's little place. The gate was shut and she peered through the iron fence at the palatial grounds. She wondered how Guin had come to live on such an extravagant piece of property even if it was only the pool house.

"Can I help you?" The voice startled her. An attractive brunette was collecting the mail for the main house. April studied her slender build, smooth glowing skin and long, silky hair. She reminded her of Demi Moore. April blinked, refocused on her task at hand.

"I was looking for Guin, but the gate's locked."

"Of course," she said. She punched a code into the system to let April onto the grounds. She walked across the lawn to meet her and together they headed toward the back of the property. "I'm Carly, and you are…?"

Carly Knowles? The actress? Her upper-handed tone made April uncomfortable. "I'm April, her partner."

"We used to be partners too. Long ago."

April had meant work partner. She hated the jealousy she was feeling and had to bite her tongue to stop herself from responding to the haughty insinuation. The woman was as much a fresh-faced stunner in person as she was under ten pounds of makeup and good lighting.

They arrived at the pool and she nodded toward the little cottage situated nearby.

"Here we are. It's a sweet little place, isn't it?"

"Yeah, it's nice."

"There's a key under the flowerpot."

"Thanks."

"No problem. And tell Guin I said hi."

She had no intention of telling Guin any such thing. She knocked but knew there would be no answer. April didn't go inside. Instead she settled onto the little stoop to wait it out, pressing redial every few minutes. She didn't blame Guin for not picking up.

Guin ditched her car in long-term parking at Bob Hope Airport and went straight to the ticket counter. Her phone rang for the twentieth time at least—again April, and again she pressed ignore and dropped it back into her jacket pocket.

"One, please. Hawaii." She decided her destination right on the spot and practically spat it out to the young Asian woman behind the counter. She'd never been to Hawaii.

"Departing when?"

"Now. Right this minute."

The woman made a few keystrokes, looked up at her. "We have a flight leaving in two hours, United. That's as right this minute as I can get you."

She drummed her fingertips on the countertop; considered revising her destination, then decided she'd wait it out in the bar. She slapped her credit card down and nodded. "Where's the lounge?"

"Down the corridor to the left. Can't miss it." The woman finished her keystrokes, bent down to retrieve the paperwork.

"Thanks." Guin took the printed boarding pass and shoved it into her pocket. Her cell phone was ringing again, and she was thoroughly annoyed. She pressed ignore and dialed Sloan's office. She was thankful it was after hours, knew she'd get a voice mail. Better to call in now than later when she'd promised herself she'd be thoroughly drunk, airline rules be damned.

She left a garbled message about being sick and needing several days off starting right away. The fact that she was an emotional wreck worked to her benefit. She sounded truly sick. She flipped the phone shut and ordered a drink to settle her nerves. She did manage to stretch three drinks over an hour. No sense in tempting the airline staff into keeping her off the flight. That would derail her entire plan for an even better drunk once she'd arrived in Honolulu.

The phone had continued to ring. Guin rolled her eyes, started to kill the power, but on impulse, answered the thing. "What the fuck do you want?"

"Maybe a little more respect than that, even if it is after hours."

Guin visibly slumped. It was Jace Sloan. "Lieutenant, I thought you were someone else."

"I sure hope so."

"Sorry, ma'am."

"Marcus, I just got your message. How are you feeling?"

"Um, I'm bad. All tired, achy."

"Uh-huh. Well, you look pretty good."

Guin stared at the phone when the call suddenly disconnected. Jace Sloan was standing a few feet away from her in the lounge entrance. She shook her head and sauntered over to join her. "How's that cough medicine?"

"What are you doing here?"

"I couldn't let you fly by yourself, when you're feeling so sick and all."

Guin slumped. "How did you know?"

"Overhead the speaker system in the background." Sloan smirked, waved at the bartender for a beer. "Unless Walgreens is having a current threat level of orange."

"Shit."

"Then I called Officer Reese who told me you two had a little falling out. The airport was just my lucky guess. And I flashed my badge and got your flight info and, of course, I knew you'd be in the closest bar."

"You're good."

"Damn right. Beer please, whatever's on tap," she told the bartender. She saw the corner of Guin's boarding pass peeking out of her pocket, snatched it up and examined it. "Well, what do you know? How about this? Your seat is right next to mine."

"What?" Guin looked at the boarding passes that Sloan had laid out on the bar top. "What'd you tell your partner this time? You were building an addition onto the house?"

"I told her exactly what I was doing, something that's called keeping the lines of communications open." Sloan scoffed. "You should try it sometime. Works like a charm."

Guin narrowed her eyes. "And she has no problem with you running off to Hawaii with another woman."

"Oh, she had a problem with it, all right." Sloan nodded in an exaggerated fashion. "She had a hell of a problem with it. But she knows I'm repaying an old debt of gratitude, and lucky for me, my partner is a big believer in honor."

Guin felt thoroughly confused. She shook her head. "What debt?"

The bartender slid a frosty mug in front of Sloan. She raised it in a one-sided toast and took a sip, then she was ready to talk. "I was abandoned when I was ten."

"I was abandoned when I was eight." Guin intended to one-up her.

Sloan furrowed her brow. "Don't interrupt me when I'm telling a story," she warned. "Anyway, somebody brought me to Heart House. Your Granny June took hold of my scrawny little arm and knew everything there was to know about me without me ever saying a word. Then she just hugged me tight and told me it was going to be all right."

Guin's sarcastic grin had faded long ago. "I didn't know..."

"Of course you didn't. I bet you don't know how special that woman is to so many people," Sloan said. "I got into a decent foster home. Granny June took a shine to me, mentored me until I was in the Academy."

"She never mentioned any of this to me." Guin pushed her empty glass aside.

"When I graduated, I told her I could never thank her for what she'd done for me. She told me I could help someone else one day and I promised I would." Sloan took a sip of beer, got quiet. "Didn't think it'd be you. But with all the pictures your grandmother was always showing me, I knew that bratty grin of yours in an instant."

Guin tipped her head to one side. "You trying to save me from myself, Sloan?"

"Somebody ought to." She took a long sip. "You already check your luggage?"

Guin shook her head. "I didn't bring any."

"That track suit is going to be a real hit on the sand."

"I don't plan on leaving my room," Guin stated factually.

"Oh hell no. You ain't going to go all *Leaving Las Vegas* on my watch." Sloan took a sip of her beer. "I didn't tell you the whole truth about April. I didn't call her. I found her at your place."

"Why did you go there?" Guin started to motion for another, but Sloan pushed her hand down, slid a glass of water her way. It was getting to be a standard between them.

"I went there to make sure you didn't take a dip in your pool and not come back up." Sloan paused. "Anyway, April told me to tell you she's sorry."

Guin stared at the glass of water before she ran her finger through the condensation. "Did she tell you that she's back with her ex?"

"She said they moved back in together this weekend."

Despite the vision, Guin was still shocked at the verbal confirmation. Her heart dropped. "She should have told me."

"Yes, she should have told you, but she didn't. And that sucks." Sloan tipped back the beer, drained it, set it back on the bar top. "But it sure sounds like she's not over you yet."

"She's with her ex. I'd say she's over me." Guin's words dripped with sarcasm.

"Maybe she wants the best of both worlds," Sloan said. She shrugged. "Wouldn't be the weirdest thing you've got going on in your life."

The reference to her talent was not lost on Guin. "Funny. No thanks."

Sloan changed the subject. "Speaking of your place. Whose big old house is that anyway?"

Guin shrugged. "Former girlfriend."

"Of course it is," she said as the bartender set another beer in front of her. "You are one busy and complicated woman, Guin Marcus."

"I'll toast to that."

"First, some ground rules before we enjoy our little recovery getaway. Number one, we're not getting our freak on, you hear?"

Guin's eyes widened. She burst out laughing. "What would make you think I'd try?"

"Of course you'd try," Sloan smirked. She waved her hand down the length of her body in demonstration. "Who wouldn't want this?"

Guin smiled, sipped her water.

"And just wait until you see my little number of a swimsuit." Sloan made a low whistle.

"I'll try to resist somehow."

"You will resist." Guin still couldn't tell if she was joking or not. "I ain't saying it's going to be easy, but you'll manage."

"Okay." She humored her friend.

"And number two; we're going to learn how to have a little fun without getting stupid drunk and chasing tail."

"You're really taking all the fun out of this vacation."

"That's what friends are for." Sloan reached across the bar and grabbed Guin's arm, gave it a squeeze. "Sometimes you just get through stuff."

Guin watched her sipping her beer. "You're a pain in the ass, Sloan."

"Why thank you, Marcus."

"No." Guin shook her head, smiled, and meant it. "Thank you."

CHAPTER TWENTY-SEVEN

Guin left the Big Island recharged with fresh, floral air in her lungs and headed back to LA. The city was recovering from a good rain and now the breeze off the Pacific was blowing ashen clouds over the hills and out to the desert. They'd be just a memory before they ever even hit the mainland. She breathed in the murky air; sickly reveled in the air quality of her favorite city.

She took a step out onto the airport crosswalk where Jace nearly mowed her down in her tiny hybrid car. Guin yanked her foot back out of the way like a kid who'd tried to get into bathtub water that was too hot. Sloan's perfectly white smile clearly showed even behind her tinted windows. She wagged her finger at Guin as Guin half-grinned, opened the passenger side door and leaned in.

"What—you can't get enough of me, Sloan?" Guin shook her head. "We just spent four days together on an island, for chrissakes."

"That hair of yours is sun-streaked as hell." Sloan shot her a look of approval. "A few days out of California and you start to look like a true Californian. Go figure."

Guin raked her hands through crazy blond ringlets. She tipped her head playfully. "You jealous?"

"Sure," she said with sarcasm. "Get in. I'll drive you to your car."

She did as she was told; hefting a new gym bag, which was considerably bulky. She'd bought everything she'd worn on the island, including underwear. She shut the door.

"I'm in the self-park lot. Clear out yonder."

Sloan veered the car away from the awning-covered walkway.

"Hey, I was thinking about something." Sloan heard Guin sigh and from the corner of her eye saw her slump slightly in her seat. "That power of yours, is it ever wrong?"

Guin started to roll her eyes and tell her how dumb an inquiry that was. But quite honestly, she didn't know for sure. Her powers seemed to be changing and growing every day.

When she didn't answer right away, Sloan elaborated. "When you were at that alarm company the first time, you pegged that tattooed boy as part of the scam. Turns out he wasn't. Weird, huh?"

She glanced in Guin's direction having successfully made her first point. Point two was on deck, and it didn't disappoint. "And when your grandmother had that vision about your old partner getting shot?—you said she didn't know exactly who it was because sometimes when it's a person close to you, you don't get the whole picture."

Perhaps they'd shared too much the past few days. As Sloan's chaperoning had deprived Guin the opportunity to behave like a total drunk, Guin had had no choice but to open up and really talk to her. But it was Guin's intention to leave all those heart-to-hearts on the island. She sighed loudly. "What's your point, Jace?"

Sloan shrugged. "Maybe it's not one hundred percent is all I'm saying."

Guin had thought about April nonstop, but her vision had been ultraclear. In fairness, it wasn't like she hadn't shared her women before, like Cheryl with her husband. But with April, she'd wanted it to be different. She'd wanted April to be all hers.

"You think I'm wrong about it?"

Another shrug. "Don't know. But you shouldn't rule it out."

"Really," Guin said, feigning indifference.

Sloan reached across the narrow seat, patted her arm. "It would be a tragedy if this was all one big visionary oops, now, wouldn't it?"

Guin mouthed the word "oops." She felt her mood take a turn toward the way of the weather. She bit her lip, didn't have anything to say. Sloan steered into the self-park lot, pulled right up behind Guin's car.

Then Guin was suddenly serious. "Thanks for...well, everything."

"That's what friends are for."

In truth, having her company had meant everything to Guin. She got out, popped the locks of her car and let the door hang open, letting pent-up heat and the smell of something not altogether right waft out. She tossed her bag into the backseat and slid behind the wheel.

Blackened, shriveled flower petals were scattered everywhere, evidence of Guin having shoved a perfectly good dozen roses out the window in anger, days earlier. She leaned over and plucked them off the seat and floorboard. When she leaned up again, her elbow brushed against the extended cup holder that still held stale half-full coffees with long-soured creamer. April had brought them out to the car the last morning they'd worked together.

She got back out of the car armed with cups and flower bits and headed for the garage trash receptacle a few feet away. She dropped in the first cup and then noticed the pale peach outline of dried lip gloss where April's lips had touched. Figuring herself a glutton for punishment, she touched it.

Like that, she was presented with a vivid image of April, naked, spooned against her in bed. Guin's own hair was sun-streaked from her impromptu vacation. She expelled a draining breath and leaned against the cement column. She took a second look at her vision. April's lips were parted in the security of sleep, Guin's arm draped snugly around her. Peaceful. Happy.

She forced herself to drop the Styrofoam cup into the garbage.

The fiasco had been as much Guin's fault as it had been April's. The visions she'd been injected with so swiftly upon meeting April were mind-blowing—she wasn't even over Cheryl yet. Yet there she was with a window into the future, knowing full and well that she and April would end up in the sack together. She had to admit that it was an unfair advantage, and as it had turned out, maybe not such an advantage after all.

Perhaps if she'd not been privy to such erotic imagery, things between them would have developed slowly, differently, and for the better. Guin had known from a simple stack of towels that April had unfinished business. Guin had unfinished business too. If April could be accused of pilfering Guin's last ounce of sanity and destroying her security, Guin could rightfully be accused of driving her getaway car about hundred miles an hour. Dammit all anyway.

She recalled other visions of April; the ones where she'd witnessed her bad breakup with Lauren and subsequent tearful meltdown in the shower. She'd so admired April's curvaceous, toned, tanned body through the shower curtain—guiltily craved her right there on the spot despite the fact that she was clearly hurting, clearly in need, so very much in pain over the breakup. And then it occurred to her.

Guin had been in both of April's apartments; the former had only a bathtub.

Had she actually forecast that event? Her mind went mad with the possibilities. Her talent or curse—whatever it was, was ever-changing, never ceased to baffle. How could she not have remembered that only April's new place had a shower? How could she have known that April was crying over…her?

Guin's mind raced with a series of potential mistakes and apologies, each one canceling out the last. She tried to assimilate a mental timeline; tried to source out the right words, but lacked experience with such things. No amount of supernatural ability would help her now. The responsibility was strictly her own— what she could feel, not what she could see, or foresee, as the case might be.

"Eyesight over insight please, Guin," she muttered to herself. She shook her head as she concluded that she'd jumped to some pretty serious conclusions based on her own watered-down, out-of-control visions.

Granny June was right. Her talent-slash-handicap had drifted out of its infancy, was refining, but was still merely in its adolescence. She could not punish everyone around because of her inability to control things just yet.

She hoped it wasn't too late.

In the car she fished her phone out of her gym bag and turned it on for the first time in three days. According to the missed alerts, April's calls had continued to come in at a frantic pace, and then ended abruptly. Apparently she'd finally given up.

But Guin had not.

Hours later, April was at Guin's door. After a strange moment, they moved toward each other and embraced. April kissed her, an action that set off a chain of events that had them clumsily headed toward the bed, fumbling with buttons and snaps. Guin forced herself to remember the reason for the reunion and drew back, breathless.

"Wait a minute," she said, leading April to the edge of the bed. They sat down. "I need to tell you something."

April looked concerned. "What is it? You can tell me anything."

Guin wasn't so sure. "Can I? Really?"

April was hesitant, but nodded. "Of course."

Guin's eyes felt sandy, her throat tight. She dove in before she could change her mind about it. "In our family...my mother..."

April seemed to feel Guin's pain. She edged nearer her, kissed her forehead, smiled sweetly. "It's okay. Take your time."

Guin started over. "Some people are born with...gifts. And

it's their parents' job to nurture and encourage those gifts, you know? So that they feel normal and special and can be productive in life."

April looked confused. "Gifted? Like in school, right?"

"No, April," Guin said, shaking her head. Her eyes begged understanding. "I need you to listen to what I'm saying instead of trying to draw your own conclusions or this will never make sense. Promise me you'll open your mind, okay?"

"Okay. I promise."

Guin took a deep breath. "I...can sometimes see things that have happened, or that are about to happen..."

"Are you telling me that you really are psychic?" April seemed to recall their weeks earlier conversation when she'd scoffed about such abilities. When Guin nodded, April looked nervous, swallowed hard, but gently encouraged her. "It's okay, I think. Go ahead."

"You're going to love this one," Guin said, taking a deep breath. "I sometimes see ghosts...and other stuff."

April seemed to take it all in. Guin nodded to confirm that she'd heard correctly. "And this runs in your family?"

"Well, I don't know my father," Guin answered, then added, "I doubt my nutty mother even knew him." She sighed and her eyes went momentarily wide indicating that she could go on forever on that subject. She resisted and continued her story. "My granny and my crazy mom and me—we all have this..."

"Is your mom really crazy?"

"Gloria is really crazy, but I doubt that has much to do with her...visions." Guin smiled and twinkled her fingers. "I do remember as a kid watching her do everything in her power to squash those images. Pills, booze, sex—lots of sex. That's how I landed on Granny June's doorstep. A few times."

April swiped a stray curl away from Guin's eyes. "How old were you?"

"Young enough to get a second shot at life, old enough to be thoroughly warped." She shrugged. "And I was having my own visions by that time, which wasn't exactly making a positive contribution to my mental health."

April looked as if she would cry. "Oh, hon..."

"Anyway, Granny June did right by me, making me only half the nut I am today instead of fully certifiable, like good old Mom." Guin glanced around nervously. "I'm going to get a drink."

"No." April stopped her from getting up. "I need to hear every bit of this unfiltered, Guin. It's important. I don't want you to hide from me."

"Okay." Guin sat back down. "Ask me anything you want."

"How do you do it?"

Guin took her time. "I touch things and I can see who was there, what happened."

"Like at the crime scene?"

"Yes," Guin quickly answered. "And other things. Like beds are the worst for me. They are ripe with energy for some reason. I know who was there, who sneaked out the morning before..." She said, chuckling softly. "Makes it hard for me to have faith in people. I always know when someone's cheated on me."

"Oh, Guin..."

She raised her eyes to April's, forced herself to get to the point. "I saw you with your ex in your kitchen, so I knew you were cheating on me."

April surprised her by nodding. "Lauren is with me, that's true. She has no other place to go. Even though she was the one who caused our relationship to unravel, I figured after that many years together, I owe her another chance. Guin, I love her and I'm faithful to her," April whispered. Her eyes were misty, her lips tipped into a tiny smile. "Problem is, that's exactly the way I feel about you."

Guin's shoulders softened. "Wow. I guess timing is everything."

"Yeah," April said, wrapping her arms around Guin. She pulled her tightly to her, kissed her.

Guin smiled as April kissed her neck. At least she knew where she stood. It had been a strange few weeks, but she felt certain everything was in its place. Her powers were evolving, growing stronger, giving her greater insight to her work than she'd ever thought possible. For once, she welcomed the clarity as opposed to drowning it in alcohol. Jace's mission had yielded more than a mere rescue, and for it, she'd made a good friend. Terence, her dear friend, was likely at that moment happily in the arms of his new love. And Granny June was probably with her bridge ladies, being herself, a beacon of generous light for which Guin aspired to both follow and emulate. It seemed possible now more than ever before.

True, April had Lauren in her life, but Guin had shared her loves before. Perhaps there was a lesson to be learned from it all. It was time to quit relying on someone else to save her from herself. Guin wondered if a dog or cat would adequately fill some of her time.

If all else failed, given the right night and the right ambience, perhaps she wouldn't be opposed to a little...haunting.

**Publications from
Bella Books, Inc.**
Women. Books. Even Better Together.
**P.O. Box 10543
Tallahassee, FL 32302
Phone: 800-729-4992
www.bellabooks.com**

CALM BEFORE THE STORM by Peggy J. Herring. Colonel Marcel Robideaux doesn't tell and so far no one official has asked, but the amorous pursuit by Jordan McGowan has her worried for both her career and her honor.
978-0-9677753-1-9

THE WILD ONE by Lyn Denison. Rachel Weston is busy keeping home and head together after the death of her husband. Her kids need her and what she doesn't need is the confusion that Quinn Farrelly creates in her body and heart.
978-0-9677753-4-0

LESSONS IN MURDER by Claire McNab. There's a corpse in the school with a neat hole in the head and a Black & Decker drill alongside. Which teacher should Inspector Carol Ashton suspect? Unfortunately, the alluring Sybil Quade is at the top of the list. First in this highly lauded series.
978-1-931513-65-4

WHEN AN ECHO RETURNS by Linda Kay Silva. The bayou where Echo Branson found her sanity has been swept clean by a hurricane — or at least they thought. Then an evil washed up by the storm comes looking for them all, one-by-one. Second in series.
978-1-59493-225-0

DEADLY INTERSECTIONS by Ann Roberts. Everyone is lying, including her own father and her girlfriend. Leaving matters to the professionals is supposed to be easier! Third in series with *PAID IN FULL* and *WHITE OFFERINGS*.
978-1-59493-224-3

SUBSTITUTE FOR LOVE by Karin Kallmaker. No substitutes, ever again! But then Holly's heart, body and soul are captured by Reyna... Reyna with no last name and a secret life that hides a terrible bargain, one written in family blood.
978-1-931513-62-3

MAKING UP FOR LOST TIME by Karin Kallmaker. Take one Next Home Network Star and add one Little White Lie to equal mayhem in little Mendocino and a recipe for sizzling romance. This lighthearted, steamy story is a feast for the senses in a kitchen that is way too hot.
978-1-931513-61-6

2ND FIDDLE by Kate Calloway. Cassidy James's first case left her with a broken heart. At least this new case is fighting the good fight, and she can throw all her passion and energy into it.
978-1-59493-200-7

HUNTING THE WITCH by Ellen Hart. The woman she loves — used to love — offers her help, and Jane Lawless finds it hard to say no. She needs TLC for recent injuries and who better than a doctor? But Julia's jittery demeanor awakens Jane's curiosity. And Jane has never been able to resist a mystery. #9 in series and Lammy-winner.
978-1-59493-206-9

FAÇADES by Alex Marcoux. Everything Anastasia ever wanted — she has it. Sidney is the woman who helped her get it. But keeping it will require a price — the unnamed passion that simmers between them.
978-1-59493-239-7

ELENA UNDONE by Nicole Conn. The risks. The passion. The devastating choices. The ultimate rewards. Nicole Conn rocked the lesbian cinema world with Claire of the Moon and has rocked it again with Elena Undone. This is the book that tells it all...
978-1-59493-254-0

WHISPERS IN THE WIND by Frankie J. Jones. It began as a camping trip, then a simple hike. Dixon Hayes and Elizabeth Colter uncover an intriguing cave on their hike, changing their world, perhaps irrevocably.
978-1-59493-037-9

WEDDING BELL BLUES by Julia Watts. She'll do anything to save what's left of her family. Anything. It didn't seem like a bad plan...at first. Hailed by readers as Lammy-winner Julia Watts' funniest novel.
978-1-59493-199-4

WILDFIRE by Lynn James. From the moment botanist Devon McKinney meets ranger Elaine Thomas the chemistry is undeniable. Sharing — and protecting — a mountain for the length of their short assignments leads to unexpected passion in this sizzling romance by newcomer Lynn James.
978-1-59493-191-8

LEAVING L.A. by Kate Christie. Eleanor Chapin is on the way to the rest of her life when Tessa Flanaghan offers her a lucrative summer job caring for Tessa's daughter Laya. It's only temporary and everyone expects Eleanor to be leaving L.A...
978-1-59493-221-2

SOMETHING TO BELIEVE by Robbi McCoy. When Lauren and Cassie meet on a once-in-a-lifetime river journey through China their feelings are innocent...at first. Ten years later, nothing — and everything — has changed. From Golden Crown winner Robbi McCoy.
978-1-59493-214-4

DEVIL'S ROCK: THE SEARCH FOR PATRICK DOE by Gerri Hill. Deputy Andrea Sullivan and Agent Cameron Ross vow to bring a killer to justice. The killer has other plans. Gerri Hill pens another intriguing blend of mystery and romance in this page-turning thriller.
978-1-59493-218-2

SHADOW POINT by Amy Briant. Madison Maguire has just been not-quite fired, told her brother is dead and discovered she has to pick up a five-year old niece she's never met. After she makes it to Shadow Point it seems like someone—or something—doesn't want her to leave. Romance sizzles in this ghost story from Amy Briant.
978-1-59493-216-8

JUKEBOX by Gina Daggett. Debutantes in love. With each other. Two young women chafe at the constraints of parents and society with a friendship that could be more, if they can break free. Gina Daggett is best known as "Lipstick" of the columnist duo Lipstick & Dipstick.
978-1-59493-212-0

BLIND BET by Tracey Richardson. The stakes are high when Ellen Turcotte and Courtney Langford meet at the blackjack tables. Lady Luck has been smiling on Courtney but Ellen is a wild card she may not be able to handle.
978-1-59493-211-3